GRIFFINTOWN

*

MARIE HÉLÈNE POITRAS

GRIFFINTOWN

* * *

A NOVEL TRANSLATED BY
SHEILA FISCHMAN

Originally published in French as Griffintown,
copyright © Éditions Alto and Marie Hélène Poitras, 2012
English translation copyright © 2016 Sheila Fischman
This edition copyright © Cormorant Books, 2016

 Canada Council   Conseil des Arts   ONTARIO ARTS COUNCIL
for the Arts   du Canada   CONSEIL DES ARTS DE L'ONTARIO
an Ontario government agency
un organisme du gouvernement de l'Ontario

 Canadian Patrimoine   Canadä
Heritage   canadien

The publisher gratefully acknowledges the support of the Canada Council for the
Arts and the Ontario Arts Council for its publishing program. We acknowledge the
financial support of the Government of Canada through the Canada Book Fund
(CBF) for our publishing activities, and the Government of Ontario through the
Ontario Media Development Corporation, an agency of the Ontario Ministry of
Culture, and the Ontario Book Publishing Tax Credit Program.

We acknowledge the financial support of the Government of Canada
through the National Translation Program for Book Publishing, an initiative of the
Roadmap for Canada's Official Languages 2013–2018: Education, Immigration,
Communities, for our translation activities.

LIBRARY AND ARCHIVES CANADA CATALOGUING IN PUBLICATION

Poitras, Marie Hélène, 1975–
[Griffintown. English]
Griffintown / Marie Hélène Poitras ; translated by Sheila Fischman.

Translation of: Griffintown.
Issued in print and electronic formats.
ISBN 978-1-77086-388-0 (pbk.). — ISBN 978-1-77086-389-7 (epub). —
ISBN 978-1-77086-390-3 (mobi)

I. Fischman, Sheila, translator II. Title. III. Title: Griffintown. English.

PS8581.O245G7413 2016   C843'.6   C2013-907901-7
C2013-907902-5

Cover design: Angel Guerra/Archetype
Interior text design: Tannice Goddard
Printer: Friesens

Printed and bound in Canada

MIX
Paper from
responsible sources
FSC   FSC® C016245
www.fsc.org

This book is printed on 100% post-consumer waste recycled paper.

CORMORANT BOOKS INC.
10 ST. MARY STREET, SUITE 615, TORONTO, ONTARIO, M4Y 1P9
www.cormorantbooks.com

Author's Dedication:

For Charlotte and Olivier
Thanks to Philippe Tessier for showing me how.

Translator's Dedication:

To Michèle Jodoin, who urged me to read
this novel — and to translate it.

What he loved in horses was what he loved in men, the blood and the heat of the blood that ran them. All his reverence and all his fondness and all the leanings of his life were for the ardent hearted and they would always be so and never be otherwise.

— CORMAC MCCARTHY, *ALL THE PRETTY HORSES*

THE BOOT

DAWN BREAKS OVER GRIFFINTOWN after months of snow and dormancy, a period of survival. Precarious sunlight appears in the east. On the horizon, in profile, a desolate landscape shot through with hills of rust where an entire genealogy of antiquated objects subsists in strata, in a doomed silence: odd hubcaps, broken bicycle chains, buckled sheets of metal. In the distance stands the royal mountain, topped by a cross, numb to the laments of the trees stretching out their bare limbs, paupers awaiting manna.

Behind the stable, the stream has thawed and its dark water is running to the canal, fresh and furious. A lot of snow fell in April. Some kindly soul has poured a little vodka into the troughs so the few remaining horses can drink when the days are cold. The constant back-and-forth between freeze and thaw has slashed severely the streets, turning them into genuine traps for calèches. Only an intimate knowledge of the days and nights of Griffintown would provide a glance at this ungrateful land of the possibility of a fertile summer.

Three horses wintered in the stable, chewing with their eroded teeth for lack of anything better than what was left of the green hay from the previous year. They have now started to rake with their hooves the scored brown soil to defy the damp indigence of spring. The scrawny animals lick big blocks of red salt, their hollow breaths warming the stable.

In the trailer parked nearby, the man keeping an eye on them has spent the last few weeks playing cribbage by himself while he waits for the night to be over and for his small heater to dry the toes of his damp boots. The man is looking for his people through the trailer's skylight. Soon he will start a count of the men and beasts winter has overwhelmed. New arrivals will occupy the loose boxes left vacant at the end of summer. Others will be returning, former runners with marks on their gums: Percherons, Belgians, bays, roans, brought back from auctions in Vermont and surroundings. The blunt rumbling of unshod hooves will once again reverberate through the stables.

Coachmen will listen to this stamping parade and they too will return to the fold embittered, poorly shod, penniless, wan-faced, and dragging their feet in tune with the animals. People always come back to Griffintown, a place where redemption is still possible. People sometimes die here too. Boots on, preferably.

✳ ✳ ✳

BILLY EXTRICATES HIMSELF FROM a dream in which — and this is rare — he was on horseback. He felt the animal's body moving under him, its warm sides stiffening under his calves, the power of the muscular machine. Gripping the pommel with one hand, he led his mount westward, beyond the limits of Griffintown, when the regular and reassuring sound of the horse's hooves trotting in the fading daylight merged with the purring of a truck engine, Paul Despatie's, followed by the animal transport vehicle occupied by new horses.

One black cowboy boot adorned with charms appears in a partly open doorway, followed by another, equally ostentatious. Paul, the man who found gold in Griffintown, owner of the stable and lord of the domain, greets his handyman and offers him a contraband cigarette. "The Indian will be back this summer," he announces. Billy nods, then they smoke in silence the musty tobacco, rolled tightly in the yellow paper.

Paul opens the doors of the transport vehicle to let the horses out. The first one appears, a ton of nerves and irritability, a raw-boned Clydesdale that will have to be fattened up before the season gets underway but who has keen eyes and a good head. Billy leads him to a stall still dominated by a card with the name of its former occupant, who was sent to the glue factory at the end of the previous summer. Jack. Billy hates to baptize animals. For convenience, he decides to call the new arrival "Jack" also, an easy name to remember, until he recalls that it's a mare — Paul said so. Billy bends under the animal to check. Taking out a pen from his shirt pocket he moistens the ballpoint and adds two letters to the end of the name: *i* and *e*. Jack becomes Jackie.

Billy makes the second mare walk to the stable, the better to note her features: fine grey-blue coat; powerful fleecy hindquarters; rather sensitive legs; the heavy grace of a Percheron but in appearance as gentle as a Belgian. She looks in vain for something cool or blooming, a tuft of weeds in all this mud, all this rust. Billy considers calling one of the new arrivals "Princess," then changes his mind. He thinks back to all the Maggies who've passed through his life as a groom: decent, proud little sweethearts — machines. He grinds his cigarette butt with his heel and slips it into his pocket as a precaution — more than anything in the world, Billy fears fire erupting in the straw. He writes Maggie on the back of a package of cigarette papers, a makeshift index card he'll put up in the stable. A name, five shovelfuls of sawdust, and a cube of hay: that's how new residents are welcomed to the stable. The blacksmith will shoe them in a few days and the veterinarian will assess their health. Then the training will begin.

Best to avoid growing attached to the horses when they arrive. Billy wouldn't have given much for the standard bred, escaped from the hippodrome afflicted by a heart murmur, but he just had to hitch the little dark horse, back this summer for an eighth season, to a light calèche and keep an eye on his hocks. He realized that Garlen Lou — yes, that's the horse's name — displayed pride inversely proportional to his height.

Like the coachmen, the horses that wash up here pull several lives behind them. They're taken as they are. For them, too, it is very often the last chance saloon.

✳ ✳ ✳

THE MEN FROM THE City have left messages repeating their offers to buy back calèche permits. The golden age has passed. Everyone knows. Even though the business is no longer as prosperous as it once was, Paul has no intention of yielding to pressure. The new owners of high-end lofts and condos don't enjoy the company of coachmen, the smells they leave behind, the pools of horse piss imprinted on the asphalt, leftover oats that crunch under the heels of their polished shoes. But the horsemen still fill their pockets with marriages.

That's how Paul gets back on his feet and fills his coffers while the coachmen blame the bad weather, fluctuations in the American dollar, or the roadwork that complicates their guided tours and scares the horses. Driving a horse and calèche through Old Montreal is a risky undertaking.

Some day — and that day is fast approaching — this tradition, and the entire legacy of coachmen's knowledge that accompanies it, will disappear. The stable, the profession, the utility of draft horses, places for them to drink. Old harnesses will disappear, as will the art of harnessing. All will end up in the museum. For now, the legend endures on faded post-cards showing passengers filled with wonder, their enthusiastic coachman with hair slicked back, a peach-coloured polo sweater knotted over his shoulders. "We're becoming fossils," thinks Paul as he sends his mail waltzing under the blades of the shredder.

When the snow melts, the lord of the domain resumes contact with the horsemen to enquire about who is coming back. He can count on a small crew of coachmen who — year in, year out — are able to get through more or less alive to the other end of the dead season. Every winter, one or two lose the duel with themselves. No one asks what has happened to So-and-So, man or horse. It's simply noted that it's no longer possible to reach one of them on his cellphone or that a new occupant has moved from one stall to another. In Griffintown, the harsh season is pitiless for those whose shadows can't be seen in the distance, whose boots or hooves can no longer be heard pounding the ground. Outside the stable, there is no salvation.

The gruff brotherhood that unites the coachmen lasts the entire season, then disappears as soon as the first leaves fall.

Then the logic of "every man for himself," of "every man against himself," reasserts itself. No one knows what will become of the drivers outside the boundaries of the territory, at night, under the snow. Fierce and merciless, winter plows their bodies, leaving them bewildered, limping through the slush, coughing loudly and spitting green while they wait for hope to return with the spring. No one talks about the absentees from the small company of horsemen, only await their return. After that, hope vanishes. For a moment they stare at the toes of their boots, then raise their heads, brows creased. Let themselves be blinded by the sun.

* * *

THIS SEASON IS OFF to a good start with John's calls. The cowboy will be with them: excellent news. John's mere presence calms the explosive nature of some, giving others the impression that, through him, justice will reign in Griffintown. John's not armed; he acts only in his own name. He became a driver seven years earlier, after a long bad spell. Unlike the new drivers, he'd known from the start how to earn the respect of the elders. He's the one who separates the men in an altercation, or stops duels, or is called on to pick up a horse that's collapsed or to finish off a dying animal. From both drivers and horses he keeps a respectful distance appreciated by all.

The sun bronzes his skin but never burns it. His gaze is hard but anyone who is able to get close to him can get a glimpse of the melancholy lapping gently in his eyes, like blue water.

At the end of every summer John hopes, on bended knee, that the season just finished is his last. But winter passes, leaving him as helpless as the other drivers. Come spring —

when Paul's voice at the other end of the line reiterates the promise of fast-made money — he hardens himself, then gives in. For most of the drivers, boarding a calèche offers salvation after falling: years of drinking, of losing everything, begging, sleeping on the steps of a church, doing time in prison, dancing nude, or working the street. For John, it's another story. He steps into a calèche like someone resuming a bad habit.

"This is my last summer, Paul," John announces.

Paul hangs up, exits his office, locks the door, lights a cigarette, and goes to the stable to join Billy.

* * *

BILLY HAS STARTED TO list the bits, leather curbs, chains, and reusable shoes in the big chest containing remnants of leather that have been thrown in every which way, along with old cracked girths, and twisted horseshoes. Paul notices that he has begun to line them up by order of size. Given the state of dilapidation of the place, trying to impose a semblance of order strikes him as absurd. Billy has his hare-brained ideas and Paul can't reproach him for anything.

When Paul inherited the stable, the groom was part of the deal, along with three scruffy old nags he had to have put down. Billy kept an eye on the premises and on the scrofulous stable of horses. Best to ensure that they're allies. At the time, he slept in the stable, at the back of the loose box where the bags of sawdust were kept. In exchange for a small weekly wage and the keys to a trailer parked between a crane and a dismantled carriage, Paul had bought Billy's loyalty; and, accordingly, a less-than-total peace of mind.

By choosing to live near the horses, the men gave up any peace and quiet because there's always something to fix, to adjust, leather to oil, filth to shovel, animals to tend, injuries to keep tabs on.... Sunny's nose was scraped, Lady limps on her right forefoot, Champion's swollen withers are starting to look like bursitis, Cheyenne and Rambo don't get along, their loose boxes in the stable should be separated — not to mention the changing temperament of Belle Starr, who has started to kick. Paul has abdicated and now lets his groom deal with these situations on his own. He devotes himself to other, less concrete problems, insidious as dormant diseases.

"Anything to do with all that scrap metal, Billy-boy?"

Some months, the groom doesn't put three words together, only cursing or spitting, at most muttering a "Hello."

"If a bit's broke you can glue it back together, but twisted, there's no way."

He has the impression he can feel his teeth shaking. Talking is at once painful and liberating, as if a bit were being taken from his mouth.

"I'll deal with that right away. I got things to do in town. Anything you need?" asks Paul. "Bolo? Chaps?"

Billy has nothing, has never had anything; he could use so many things — first of all socks, without holes, maybe a shirt or two.

"Bring me a bottle of something strong."

"Okay. By the way, John's coming back. Evan, too. He's bringing two new horses tomorrow."

Evan. The one who'd met a Windigo and has never got over it. His return does not augur well.

After putting the crate of broken bits in the back of Paul's truck, Billy watches the pickup's tires spin in the revolting mix of mud and manure. As soon as the earth has dried he'll be able to order a load of gravel before the season gets under way. Paul gives him a quick wave; he jerks his chin in return.

It's the last time he will see his boss alive.

* * *

A NUMBER MIGRATE WEST. Aside from the drivers and the horses, Evan, Le Rôdeur, and La Grande Folle head for Griffintown. Every spring, people who gravitate around them — errand boys, new drivers, blacksmiths, loan sharks — also advance towards the stables in a rickety procession. Rumour has it there is still gold to be found.

Evan crosses the first of the territorial limits.

Billy frowns when he hears in the distance squealing tires and the latest pop hit spat out at top volume. The groom feels a pang when he spots Evan driving a truck with a trailer that can hold the horses. Behind the wheel, Evan executes tricky manoeuvres. He turns with a jolt so that, at one point, truck and trailer form a right angle. The clattering procession comes within inches of overturning. When the demivolt is finished, Billy tells the horses apart by their rumps: Poney, a bay with coppery glints, and Pearl, a Percheron draft mare, one of the most beautiful in Griffintown, a mirage of black velvet and starry eyes, a short range stride but a supple jazzy step.

Billy doesn't greet Evan, who returns the favour. He notices that the face of Paul's assistant is emaciated, his jaw rigid, and his movements abrupt. He lets him sort things out on his own. Right away, Poney recognizes the stench of the place, the age-old mix of mouldy grime and sour urine along with the musty smell of the canal behind the stable — slimy water where no horse has ventured to drink. The foul smell of the three-legged cat's piss and the odour of the groom's sweat and soot rise in gusts, tempered fortunately by the dry and reassuring bouquet of sawdust. That foul fragrance clings to clothing, never to be dislodged; only fire could get rid of it thoroughly. Poney is at home here. A little later in the day he'll meet up with his colleagues, Rambo and Lucky, and just as veterans of a factory exchange a nod, he will greet them with a whinny.

In her corseted gown, La Grande Folle too is heading for the Far Ouest, a parasol protecting her from the morning light. Her high heels give her a sore back but elegance has its price; wearing them, it's easy for her to stand out in the fray. In the bottom of her handbag, all jumbled together, are a makeup kit, rubber gloves, a sponge for polishing the calèches, precious pebbles, and lots of other shameful treasures. She taps them with a long ruby nail and continues on her way.

* * *

IT HAPPENS AT THE start of every season, when a few tender-feet will come to try their luck in Griffintown. From the moment the apprentices stop their calèche driver's course at the Institut d'hôtellerie, there are some twenty desperadoes in all: two delinquents in rehab; some early retirees trying to come up with a country hobby; a dancer who'd put her back out and now carries a pillow with her everywhere; identical twins whose father was a driver; a barmaid; an exceptional student who plans to study veterinary medicine in California at the end of summer; two dyslexics who demand in loud voices an exemption from the written exam; a handicapped man in a wheelchair; several riders yearning for a horse; and, at the very bottom of the class, Marie, who one day will be called "the Rose with a Broken Neck," whose destiny will be tragically linked with that of Griffintown.

The class is divided in two parts: first, the lecture in which future drivers are taught the history of the city; some key dates; notions about architecture they'll be quick to forget; and second, equine anatomy. All apprentices wait impatiently for the start of the practical part of their training, experience to be gleaned on the ground, acquired in the driver's seat or the hand on the shoulder of a horse with its nose plunged deep in the barrel of oats, soiling the drivers' boots in the stable. The one explanation that matters most. The drivers' course lasts two months, including the final examination, with a view to obtaining a permit to drive a horse-drawn vehicle.

Generally, after visiting the stable, the group is decreased by half. The baby boomers on the verge of retirement take to their heels when they observe the sorry state of the premises. Sensitive souls take off with the same haste former coachmen do the final sorting, bringing along the newcomers with barely concealed bad faith. Simple math explains the sour reception: they are paid by the trip. More drivers, fewer trips. The cohort of newcomers, usually friendlier and interested in informing the tourists who climb on board, with better hygiene, attract more customers than the old ones. As there is no money to be made in May, contributing to the training of newcomers brings in a small sum, enough to repay La Mouche for debts accumulated before the official start of the profitable season, which always turns out better — as is well-known — with no broken arms or fractured shoulders.

✳ ✳ ✳

OTHER DRIVERS CONTINUE TO arrive. The Indian has reached the northern boundary of Griffintown. To the east, Roger and Joe are walking briskly to be among the first to choose a horse and a calèche. From every direction they are gaining ground: Georges, Lloyd, and Robert in the west, Christian and Gerry in the north on the Indian's trail. Others follow, spitting, coughing, cursing, hoping. This procession marches past accordingly, noisy, hands held out in front, all under the eye of La Mouche, an old crook with a twisted smile who, from the roof of a warehouse, casts disapproving looks on the comings and goings of those who will cling, feet and hooves, to Griffintown. The moneylender watches the arrival of one person in particular. It is said that the person who put Paul Despatie on the throne of Griffintown has disappeared, that she joined Mignonne in death. But La Mouche doesn't believe a word.

He senses her presence.

✳ ✳ ✳

THE FAR OUEST ALSO includes the old city, a tourist neighbour-hood that's more and more residential. For the drivers it's the proscenium, a site for performance and parade, one where it's wise to straighten your spine and play your character well. At the end of the day you go behind the stage, to the run-down backstage, a zone with its own founding myths and laws, where a person can drive in peace, whip in hand, a beer between the legs. Going back to the stables under the rose-coloured sky of July after a profitable day trotting along William Street makes the life of a driver acceptable. Closer to the heart of Griffintown, the hum of the city fades; at the patched-up tin castle, the skyscrapers form nothing but a string of starry shadows in the distance.

A railroad goes by in the southwest and not far from there lies the canal and all its tributaries, including the stream of sooty water that runs behind the stable and onto the bridge that joins the Far Ouest and Pointe-Saint-Charles.

At the end of the day the drivers unhitch their horses and cool them with a shower, dry them with a scraper, then confine them to rest in their stalls, where a cube of hay and blessed peace await. Unlike saddle horses to be ridden — that sleep standing up with eyes half-closed, resting one leg at a time — calèche horses lie on the ground, collapse, exhausted, their heavy eyes tightly closed, to dream of being unharnessed, of grazing or of rolling in the snow.

* * *

THE FAR OUEST HAS as many errand boys as stands: ghostly coachmen, former drivers who haven't won the battles with their demons. When a driver has to be away for a few minutes, the errand boy keeps an eye on his horse. If the moon is bright enough, which is to say rarely or never, he might board customers while they wait for the driver to return. At noon, the errand boys go out to fetch sandwiches in exchange for a few coins; the better their tips the less they tend to get lost along the way or to make mistakes in the orders. Now and then, once or twice during the season, Paul is given the task of counting the drivers' rides to see if the amount they declare at the end of the day corresponds to the true number of rides. The errand boy is a humble and mischievous individual, the joker in a card game, who takes his little job very seriously, clinging to it as to a lifeline. Sometimes the dark side surfaces and an errand boy disappears for a few days, a few weeks, coming back more wilted than before, morose, despondent, silent, and motionless, holding a can of beer, unwilling to do any favours, but present all the same. During those moments a driver offers him a sandwich.

The longest-serving of all the errand boys is a well-known tramp. With his long grey hair, his gold teeth, and his perpetual road department jacket, ripped off from a blue-collar worker, Le Rôdeur has been hanging around Griffintown longer than most of the drivers. He left the Far Ouest before the end of the last season, on all fours like a horse. Billy saw him limp towards the east along the railway track with a severe cough, clearing his throat as if breathing his last. It would have taken a clever chimney sweeper to get rid of all the soot that lined his larynx. He was at death's door. Winter may well spell the end of him and the night will cover his broken body with its shroud. Had Le Rôdeur already joined Mignonne?

That is the sad prospect Billy envisages, sitting on the roof of his trailer, when he notices in the stream where they drown kittens an object that is both familiar and no longer in use. A boot. Coming down from his perch and approaching the stream, he recognizes the boot, which is drifting on the surface of the troubled waters, at its heel a long trail of weeds. He uses a branch to get it. The boot belongs to his boss.

Squinting, Billy looks around suspiciously. In the blue-tinged, shadowy light that envelops the stable, La Grande Folle's grotesque and terrifying silhouette stands out on the wall. Shoulder against a beam in the garage, a cigarette in one hand, brandishing the garden hose above a cauldron with the other, she has kept on her feathered hat and is now posing in the twilight, all seven feet of her if you include her show-girl's headgear. To Billy's eyes she seems straight out of a dreary, degenerate theatre.

* * *

GEORGES HAS HIS EYE on the Clydesdale and the forest-green buggy. He informs Billy what he intends to do and asks where Paul has gone, but no one knows. Maybe he's crossed the border in search of new horses? Impossible to say just now; Paul Despatie does not deign to answer his messages.

The coachman starts to decorate the calèche, tying plastic vines and roses and stuffed teddy bears to the roof. He stows a blanket in the rear trunk and scatters some trinkets under the driver's seat to show others that the calèche has already been spoken for. Then he steps into the stall of the big bay horse he covets and urinates into the straw to mark his territory.

That year, Lloyd is also among the first to drag his carcass to Griffintown. Even though it's a little early to get the season underway, the driver seems anxious to harness the horses, probably because of debts run up at the end of the previous, disastrous summer he'd drowned in alcohol. In August he'd got into the habit of turning up at the stable in the morning, eyes already glassy and speech confused, staggering and expressing himself in a franglais impossible to decode. After noon at the calèche stand, Lloyd passed out in his horse's diaper and the animal made his way to the stable on his own. Paul had let the driver go before the end of the season and Lloyd, out of ideas, had resigned himself to making a deal with the moneylender. To repay his debt to La Mouche was becoming urgent.

Over the years Lloyd has become attached to a big blackish-brown mare with a nervous temperament he called Charogne or carrion, a former racehorse with tattoos on the neck just under the mane, which is fine and glossy. The tattoo was a dream of the driver who would have preferred to become a jockey.

The spotted Appaloosa is reserved for the Indian and always has been; they're a winning combination and all the rage among European tourists. A cream-coloured palomino waits quietly for the return of Robert. The horse is impossibly coloured maiden's blush, built like a little buffalo, watching from the corner of her eye for Gerry to arrive. The old horses — Champion, Majesty, Luck — are reserved for tenderfeet because they are calm, practically deaf, horribly slow, and thus less inclined to cause accidents. They are just as reassuring.

* * *

THE TENDERFEET WILL SOON arrive in Griffintown, but Paul is delayed. Something's out of place, like a horseshoe landing crooked on the ground. Billy has spent a lot of time brooding on the roof of his trailer, keeping an eye on the stream while waiting for his boss, or at the very least his left boot.

He recalls conversations he's had with Paul, when the other man appeared exhausted, sick of pulling Griffintown's strings. Paul has let it be understood that he sometimes has an urge to give it all up and make a new life for himself by the ocean in the South, far from the horses, even farther from the drivers. Billy has never taken it seriously; after all, he too was sick and tired of riffraff. But he has a tough hide. Maybe without knowing it he'd ignored an alarm signal. Maybe Paul is driving down Route 66 and where he's going he'll never need cowboy boots again. So why did he drop just one in the stream?

* * *

ONE MORNING, AFTER HE'S fed the horses, Billy hitches up Maggie and goes to a print shop on the outskirts of Griffintown to make a wanted poster using an old photo of Paul. Wanted: Man wearing one boot, railway track tattoo on arm and possibly a bullet hole. Wanted dead or alive. Ransom offered $$$.

Thinking it's a joke or a setup, the employee smiles until the sight of the man standing at the counter makes him change his mind. Faded jeans, genuine cowboy boots, John Deere cap, contraband cigarette stuck to his lips; no doubt about it, this is a genuine desperado.

The photo, dog-eared and yellow, shows a serene Paul smoking a cigarette on the square opposite the Basilica, in front of his finest buggy, the one shaped like Cinderella's coach, hitched to Mignonne. Billy remembers as if it were yesterday. He'd snapped the photo a while before but for once, his boss appears happy. Totally different from the troubles that have been making his life miserable in recent times.

Outside, a delivery man is honking his horn; the calèche is parked in the wrong place. Seeing that Maggie has folded her ears, stiffened her hindquarters and begun to stamp the ground, annoyed, Billy rushes to pay the bill and leaves with a hundred posters under his arm. On the way home he slaps them onto every telephone pole.

The smile of Paul Despatie, repeated a hundred times like an appeal, like an unintelligible omen. Or a bad joke.

✳ ✳ ✳

MARIE STILL HAS TROUBLE believing there are horses in the city. In her mind they still belong in the country, where she had to leave them behind when she chose to live in the metropolis. The years spent in the big city haven't quelled the wild, physical desire to ride horses; to approach them, befriend them, rest her shoulder against theirs, lay her hand on their noses and slide it towards their warm breasts. Those movements remain etched in her and ask to blossom again. A simple stamping in the distance revives that memory and makes it crackle.

One day when she was on her way to the old city, Marie noticed horses pulling calèches and wondered where the stables were. Driven by an urge to spend some time there, she signed up for a calèche drivers' course. The rest followed in a quick and strangely concrete way. She had never set foot in Griffintown. She felt at once excited and vulnerable, suspected that the stable she was about to enter would be nothing like the riding schools she attended in the past. More than anything, she feared horses suffering because of human error.

Walking on Griffintown's scarred streets with the other tenderfeet, Marie notices the Wanted poster on the telephone poles. She feels as if she's on a film set: the air vibrates softly and something misty and volatile floats there, gold dust mixed with powdered rust. The tenderfeet feel slightly suffocated but they'll have to learn to live with the smell if they want to become drivers. Then, in a blind alley forgotten by God and man, the stable appears set in a crude patch. The smell is becoming unbearable and the putrid fumes so challenging that Marie, though she's accustomed to the smell of a stable, has tears in her eyes and begins to cough.

Arrival on the premises is by way of a swamp of shit and mud that's called the parking lot. She is aware of the suction effect around her boot, the inelegant and ugly sound that accompanies it, and it amuses her until she can't extricate herself and begins to sink in. Billy comes to her rescue. By way of thanks, Marie offers him one of the peppermints intended for the horses. He sticks the candy in his mouth, revealing blackish stumps. The decrepitude here has poisoned even the teeth of the groom.

The stable is partly occupied by draft horses, giants squeezed into tiny stalls. First pain. Taking advantage of the group's departure to check out the premises, Marie puts her palm on Pearl's black crupper, making her flinch, surprised. From that first contact, the mare is aware of a benevolent tremor. Then Marie makes her way to her flank and they peer at one another. She puts a green apple on the cube of hay, breaking it into two equal parts with her thumb in an unconscious gesture she has repeated a thousand times. The mare makes short work of it while Marie sticks her hand into its watering trough to get rid of the dirt lodged there: a stem of hay, some pigeon fluff, a tangle of grimy filaments and cobwebs. She lets the water run until it's clear and notices a scratch running down the creature's nose; she vows that she will take care of it. Half-heartedly, the mare takes advantage of Marie's proximity to see if by chance there were some sweets in her pocket. She finds a few pink candies and munches them, satisfied. Marie plunges her face in the animal's long mane and inhales deeply.

"Looking for work?" Billy has observed the scene. If this girl worked for Paul the horses would be in good hands.

"Yes, I've signed up for the driving course. I'd really love to work here."

"Fantastic. You start in two days. I'm Billy."

At once disarmed and amused by the turn of events, Marie gets ready to rejoin the group when suddenly her attention is captured by the sight of a horse with a greyish-brown coat waiting patiently to be harnessed. John appears with the harness and a kettle of feed.

"Beautiful animal," observes Marie.

John isn't very fond of humans, especially the new drivers. He can't stand their lack of know-how, thinks their ignorance is dangerous. And this little girl is way too pretty to be working on a calèche.

Marie slides her thumb to the corner of the horse's lips to check the enamel of the gelding's teeth and determine his age. Reflexively, he pulls open the mouth.

"I'd say he's eight or nine. A beautiful horse but he's badly shod. You can see that where the pastern is swollen."

That's a girl who knows horses. John can see right away

that she knows her way around a horse, though she's not the kind who claims to know everything and spends hours grooming hers in the stable but ends up wearing him out from asking too much of him. Little girls are demanding and may seem pitiless; he knows this only too well. The previous summer he and Billy had to use firecrackers to help Lucky get to his feet after a young woman driver had pushed him too far. Horses give all they've got, far more from bravery than from pride, then they collapse, broken. Small, precious, cavalier despots; John loathes them.

In a concert of clacking dry leather and metal knocking together, the driver tightens the girth, pushes back the mare to face the calèche, adjusts the breeching strap, checks the angle of the reins, ties off the last braids, hoists herself onto the driver's seat, grabs hold of a long riding crop.

"Squeeze in there if you don't want your foot run over by a hoof or a wheel."

In the man's eyes there is something harsh and ravaged, the hollow echo of a field of ruins. Marie takes one step back.

✳ ✳ ✳

LATE THE FOLLOWING AFTERNOON, when two or three horses are waiting in the alley to be hitched up for the night rounds, the drone of a big truck with a tired engine can be heard.

"Billy!" barks Lloyd, fixing a bag of oats for Charogne. "Here's your shitload of gravel!"

Without leaving his cab the driver pours a mountain of grey rocks right next to Cinderella's coach. Armed with a rake and a shovel, Billy begins as he does every summer to hide the tainted pudding that covers the ground.

For the veteran horses, the sound announces more comfort. Stone dust absorbs half the surrounding mugginess, tempers the air in the stable, offers a climate that's better for wrecked joints and sensitive hocks.

For Billy, covering the surrounding blemishes, shovelling stones over shit, is the activity that comes closest to a spiritual practice, along with rolling pennies. He does it every year, praying silently for abundance to come to Griffintown and for suffering and malevolence to stay away. He prays for the horses to be solid on their hooves, for the drivers to stand firm and not wobble, for Paul to come back, for Evan to disappear ... for the radio to stop screeching! He's going to punch it and go back to his task, letting gratitude sweep over him. "Thanks for the bed and the shelter where they let me sleep. Thank you for the Chinese boy who deliveries soft drinks, instant coffee, onions, and ground beef. Thank you for good health, in spite of toothaches. Thank you, I'm on my feet and grateful."

Grey above the blackish purée, a tiny clink of gravel like a bell to announce school will start again, sounding the possibility of a fresh start.

The air is mild, the stable peaceful and clean, nearly all the stalls occupied; in the fridge, some leftover shepherd's pie and cans of Dr. Pepper wait for Billy. He starts to hum a song of which he remembers half the lyrics. He mispronounces the words but he stays in tune.

The small stones muffle the putrid fumes; at last the season for the calèches can begin.

✳ ✳ ✳

ON THE VERGE OF daybreak, after drifting for nearly a week, Paul is the last to cross the limits of the territory feet first. La Grande Folle finds him near the stream, on his side like a drunk collapsed in an impossible position.

La Grande Folle touches his shoulder and, sensing the worst when there is no reaction, rolls him onto his back. Paul turns to her a martyr's face, complexion leaden. His features are bloated, his body soaking wet, purple marks around his wrists and two red holes at his heart.

She lets out a long cry, her voice wavering strangely between a man's hoarse sound and a woman's falsetto, falls silent. Never taking her eyes off the corpse, La Grande Folle steps back to Billy's trailer where he is already putting on his boots.

"Paul is dead!" shrieks the bird of ill omen, pointing at the black water. Her makeup is running, a treacherous shadow covers her temples and chin.

"Take the dress off and give me a hand," Billy orders, his jaw clenched.

They hoist the corpse into a wheelbarrow. Paul's body is folded like a pair of scissors and his hands and feet, rigid and streaming wet, stick out. Billy recalls that in the cellar there's a huge freezer where Paul used to preserve the ducks and deer he hunted in the fall. Panic-stricken, the groom gets the idea of placing the remains there; he would have to act fast. From the freezer they take a moose hock and a partridge, then stow Paul's corpse, which will remain there until they find a more dignified burial place.

The owner has been eliminated. The order of things, until now unchanging, has just been overthrown. There will be questions of honour to be weighed, maybe a revenge to be orchestrated, and probably a message to be decoded. The horsemen will have to re-establish some kind of justice and impose it. As a rule, police don't come to the Far Ouest; the authorities let the horsemen deal with these matters among themselves — as long as their stories don't go beyond the boundaries of the territory.

What happens in Griffintown stays in Griffintown; that's always been the way.

The murder is signed, its author meaning to be known; what did he want to do to the horsemen? Billy never tried to stay in the know about what was brewing behind the scenes; he was content with running the stable, which was quite enough. Today, he is sorry he didn't try to know more.

In the stable, the horses are hungry.

THE SECOND BOOT

UPRIGHT AND GAPING, AS dark as an enigma, Paul's boot sits on the table in the place of honour, next to the jar of instant coffee. The leather stiffened as it dried and is now rippled like cardboard. Billy has made the coffee strong this morning; he sweetens it generously, and while sipping this watery brew, he thinks about the death of his boss. For the groom it's a personal matter.

He remembers a film he saw years before with a cowboy on the lam who'd hidden his weapon in the very bottom of his boot and used it to lure a wealthy businessman. Spotting the boot through the window of a train, the businessman had deduced that a bandit who'd taken refuge on the train's roof was trying to find a way to get inside. He watched silently, intently, finger on the trigger of a revolver, not knowing that the mouth of a cannon was nestled in the welt of the boot. There were two holes in his forehead before the man understood what was happening to him.

Billy plunges an arm into Paul's boot, takes out something powdery — a sheaf of dried-out couch grass. Better than a drowned kitten.

The sound of tires crunching over gravel breaks into his contemplation: La Grande Folle has called a taxi. Rather than put back on the crinoline and the rustling skirt that make up the bottom of her femme fatale's gown, she has on jogging pants. With her girdle, the flesh-coloured thong that climbs up her narrow thighs, and her feathered toque, she looks like an angel fallen into disgrace. La Grande Folle belongs to the night. Dawn slows down her metamorphosis, displays her man's features, the beginnings of a beard; it reveals his male features and his false eyelashes.

Billy doesn't know much about La Grande Folle, only that she was once the cellmate of his friend Ray, the groom who now rests in peace between a patch of thistles and a heap of scrap metal, under a makeshift stone on which can be read the following epitaph: Died with his boots on. Next to Ray, beneath a cross, lies the big shattered body of Mignonne-la-Blanche. The Griffintown graveyard is home to just those two. In the secrecy of the earth, the skeletons of Ray and Mignonne are united. Both died in the stable. The other drivers and horses will pass away more discreetly, in the out-skirts of the Far Ouest, in places without a soul where even the hooves are silent.

While he plucks the partridge taken from the freezer, Billy wonders how to dispose of Paul's remains. He skewers the bird but doesn't know what else to do with it.

✳ ✳ ✳

GEORGES IS THE FIRST person to whom Billy announces the boss's death. He tells him in the harness shed. The star driver frowns, looks down. The angle of his cheekbones takes shape, becomes briefly striking, then relaxes. Men of few words, both are silent; they go down to the cellar, backs bent so they won't hit their heads. As a precaution, Billy has locked the freezer using a padlock that hangs at the end of a twisted chain and has secretly stowed a loaded shotgun behind the freezer next to the mousetrap. After making sure the gun is still there, he opens the lid of the freezer. It takes Georges's breath away. He recovers, then unexpectedly, he kneels to pray. Crosses himself, gets up. Before he goes back up the ladder, he confides to the groom:

"If I get my hands on whoever did that I'll rip his stomach open with a hoof pick and make him gobble his own guts."

* * *

A PROCESSION OF DRIVERS sombre with grief files down to the cellar all day long. Most observe silence and lower their gaze before the body, folded like a pair of scissors. Others mutter a long series of oaths. Evan, Paul's assistant, is astonishingly silent, helpless for a good three minutes. Then he points to Paul as if he wanted to fight with the other man and lets out:

"You can't do that to me!"

He delivers the freezer a good hard kick and climbs up the ladder, limping slightly.

* * *

AT THE HÔTEL SALOON the prevailing darkness contrasts with the radiance of spring. Inside, night persists, less opaque than just after dusk. Two p.m. and the place is crammed with drivers who are arguing, and spluttering. One has already fallen out of his chair, twice.

The place is run by Dan, a cousin of Paul's. A manager boasting legendary composure, always dressed to the nines: bartender's vest, bowtie around his neck. Over the years Dan has served countless pitchers of horse piss to customers, most of them regulars. The success of the place is due partly to the fact that Griffintown is dry, as they say, meaning that no business in Verdun is authorized to serve alcohol. It's said that Marguerite d'Youville, who had made a bad marriage that united her with an erratic drunk who devoted himself to trading eau-de-vie with the Natives, had handed over that part of the territory on condition the Law of Temperance be applied, banning taverns, clubs, and bars — and the sale of alcohol. Mother Marguerite headed the congregation of Soeurs Grises, grises (i.e. tipsy) because the bad reputation of François d'Youville had tainted them. She had decided that no one would be grise in Verdun any more, save the sisters.

Things are much different in Griffintown now. The Saloon is very close to a Métro station and a few strides from the stables. They serve beer, chips, pickled eggs, beef tongue, and roast beef on Friday. It didn't take long for the place to become a hangout for a motley crew of workers from a nearby factory that made multi-coloured plastic suitcases: Anglophones of Irish descent, Polish immigrants, and coachmen. Other distinctive signs: close to the entrance is a post for tying up the horses as well as a drinking trough: entrance is through swinging doors; the front is adorned with three small holes made by stray bullets and on a shelf inside stood several jars of banana peppers that have never made anyone's mouth water. They lend colour to the green marble of the walls and accumulate dust. But more than anything the soul of the place is the head and shoulders of Boy on the wall between the unisex washrooms and the counter where Dan polishes the beer glasses. On a small plaque you can read R.I.P. Boy, Norm's first horse. Norm is Paul's father, Normand Despatie, who died at the age of thirty of pneumonia. He'd had time to set up the business in Griffintown and to bring a plow horse from the Beauce: Boy, the founding horse. The matte patina of his hair and the dried matter around his eyes show that he has watched over the small society of horsemen for years and years. For so long, to tell the truth, that no one notices his presence.

But they all would have howled if anyone had dared to take him down. Boy's mounted head is treated with a deference like that reserved for statues of the Blessed Virgin in the Notre-Dame Basilica, or the monument on Place d'Armes in memory of Chomedey de Maisonneuve. It's no longer noticed, but it's reassuring to know it's still there. When he learns of his cousin's death, Dan's attitude is unchanged. He merely undoes the bow tie that suddenly is squeezing his throat, pours himself a big glass of horse piss, sits on a stool at the bar, and chugalugs his beer.

Then, all afternoon and late into the night, the drivers drink hard and argue loudly, recalling good times with Paul and memories of horses ridden in the old days. They use that time to shed light on certain legends and make a start on new ones. They invent ways to torture the person or persons who bumped off Paul, plans that involve their horses: legs and arms attached to four heavy Percherons and the spectacular quartering that would follow. Then, abruptly, the drivers fall silent; something in this story is fleeing between their fingers. Alcohol eases the torments for a few hours but the next day — aided by a hangover — worries, agitation, and something like an appetite for revenge will stir in them.

They ought to meditate, pray in silence beneath the mounted head of Boy, give proof of humility. But it's too late. Paul remains bent double in the cellar, one floor below his desk, face leaden, body increasingly rigid, frozen in an impossible torsion at the back of a padlocked freezer, with vermin reproducing all around it. Who could have committed this act that cannot be undone, and, in doing so, shattered the order and the hierarchy of the Far Ouest?

The blow was meant to be fatal. The man who ran the business had been attacked. But the horsemen have hides like leather; it will take more to scatter them. Order will come back to Griffintown.

* * *

THE DOOR TO PAUL'S office is locked. Billy will have to see about that, too. He doesn't know where to start. He considers buying a dog, a pit bull — an animal that's prompt and swift, with a fine, discriminating ear — to guard the premises when he's asleep. He rejects that idea: he already has enough animals in his care. Besides, he only shuts one eye to sleep.

Standing in the kitchen near the microwave, Billy is waiting for his frozen meal to be ready when he hears sounds on the Basin Street side, to the west: a car door opens, then closes. He steps discreetly into the sitting room, wraps himself in the curtain, and then, like a sentinel on duty, waits. His heart is pounding. He wishes he hadn't left the weapon in the cellar, behind the freezer. It's idiotic; he ought to keep it within reach. With a muted and drawn-out rumbling, a Mercedes with tinted windows drives past the stable like an eel carried by the current in a river.

"Scrounging, eh, troublemaker?" says John as he enters the living room.

Billy jumps, then is relieved to see that it's only John. A complex equation with multiple unknowns fills his thoughts. It's heavy to bear; he needs peace and quiet. He could not, for instance, tolerate the presence of Evan.

In the dangerous streets of Griffintown it's rare to see vehicles other than the drivers' jalopies, heavy dump trucks filled with straw, hay or loose stones, Paul's pickup, to which a trailer was sometimes attached …. Paul's truck! Where could it have been abandoned?

"Nearly all the calèches are at the wall. What's going on?" asks John.

He has to be put in the know too, taken down to the cellar. With a sigh, Billy invites John to follow him into the darkness.

* * *

THE NEXT DAY, THE first in her new life as an aspiring driver, Marie has cleaned out the displays in an equestrian shop and brought back a curry comb, a stiff brush, a miraculous balm that heals injuries and makes hair grow back on scars, a revitalizing cream to untangle the long manes, elastics for tying manes, a hoof pick, and sponges. She also has an expensive ointment to care for and nourish the frogs battered and bruised by the horses' hooves, an applicator brush, and a gallon of Absorbine Jr. to relieve the animals' aching hocks.

At the thought of being reunited with the horses, her heart pounds in her ribcage as if to extricate itself; Marie feels it beating all the way to her temples. She spends the evening on the little balcony, reviewing her notes, while her ex cleans out the apartment. The breakup, provoked by Marie, is as fresh as an open wound. He demonstrated he was wounded and angry, which was fine with her. He did not approve of Marie's new career choice. He was judgmental and talked more and more about going back to live in the suburbs. A world had insinuated itself between them, already driving them apart: the rough, magnetic world of horsemen. Rough.

After telling Marie he'd be back shortly with his brother to pick up the appliances and the rest of his things, he slams the door. Marie closes her eyes and sees herself emerging from her body with heady fluidity. While one part of her passes out, is dissolved in the air as fine particles, something like an ancient ego, holding reins that have been too short for too long, is reborn. There is something timid, and at the same time fearsome about her, a wild fibre, an unwillingness to accommodate herself to the civilized world she's had to muzzle in order to function well in society. One part of her could be revived. But this other part would be restored in the company of horses. The drivers struck her as unappealing and as ill-adapted as herself, even more so. Marie could finally shed her attitude of fake civility. Everyone would see behind the wilted mask a little face with distinguished features and equine eyes. By associating with the horses, a strange alchemy has forged the resemblance.

She is hungry for a new world, seeks a way to gain access to it. She will find it even though tenderfeet aren't welcome in Griffintown.

✳ ✳ ✳

MARIE LEAVES HER BIKE in the thistles. Three calèches leave the stable hitched to horses, one of which makes her smile: white, with the appearance of angora, a strange head and chaotic mane, pulling a garishly kitsch pink carriage, being driven by a man in a foul mood. May isn't a busy month for calèche rides and it's right now that, peacefully at first, the season gets underway. The drivers are content with short days; they go home, giving the horses time to recuperate from their efforts before summer really comes.

Overawed, Marie heads for the stable to begin her first day of training. As soon as she is holding the reins, it will be in the bag. Or so it seems to her.

Billy, her contact, seems to be snowed under. He executes a dance punctuated by creaking leather and the distressing symphony of scraping wheels. He harnesses the horses, tightens the girth, and coordinates the deployment of men and animals.

Her gaze sweeping the premises, Marie recognizes the twins from the drivers' course who are giving a horse a shower and saying "Hi." Two other aspiring drivers have arrived as well: an easy-going man of fifty or so and another, younger, who looks as lost as she does. Amid the hubbub of the departing calèche and the arrival of new horses no one pays them the slightest attention. Marie makes her way to the groom.

"Hi, Billy. I'm here for my training."

He takes the time to look her over from head to toe; Marie's hair is pulled into a bun and she has on a flowered skirt. She looks more like someone on her way to a piano lesson than someone who drives a calèche.

"Go with Alice," the groom stammers between dead teeth.

In one corner, a fiftyish woman is bandaging a short-legged chestnut draft horse. She has a straw hat over a long braid. Slightly apart from the others, she is taking her time. Marie notices on the bench of her calèche a big bag of carrots. This detail reassures her.

"Bonjour. Are you Alice?" she asks hopefully.

The woman bursts out laughing. Suddenly Marie has a sense that they're making fun of her.

The driver tells the others what has just happened and there is an explosion of laughter, slapped thighs, and busted guts. Even Billy, amid the storm of comings and goings he coordinates, takes a moment to laugh at Marie.

"I'm Trudy," says the driver. "Alice is the tall skinny one over there."

* * *

ALICE IS ON HIS cellphone, bawling somebody out. He hangs up, asks Billy if his calèche will be ready soon, lights a cigarette. Marie eyes him contemptuously, discouraged. The thought that she could give up this new venture, leave forever this unfriendly world, and go back home brushes against her. She takes refuge for a moment in the stable on the flank of Pearl, her only benchmark; she emerges a few minutes later and heads, not quite so determined, towards the shed.

"So, are you a boarder or a coward?" asks Alice.

Standing in a wooden calèche hitched to a black horse, sporting a mullet and a sleeveless jean jacket, Alice could just as easily be the devil in person, opening a door for her that goes straight to hell. With no hesitation, Marie gets in.

With her rear squeezed in next to Alice's on the driver's

bench, she tries to strike up a conversation by showing some interest in the horse. After two minutes of forced bench-sharing, Alice seems exasperated. "No, I don't know his name, or his age, or his breed," he replies, sorry to have let Marie get in with him. "For ten years I drove Mignonne, the finest mare in Griffintown, the most beautiful, the bravest. She's dead now. I couldn't care less about the other nags."

"I understand; it's like a broken heart."

Alice frowns. "No, you don't understand."

"Can I hold the reins?" pleads Marie with a beginner's zeal.

"Are you nuts? One thing at a time. You're going too fast!"

In the vibrant May sunlight, on Ottawa Street, a grey, windowless warehouse with a charming pink door stands out from the other storerooms. Marie wants to know what's inside but, checked by her cantankerous teacher, she swallows her question. On the left, hitched to Charogne, Lloyd passes them without a glance. Marie feels her speeding up. She doesn't know if it's because of Alice's pride or the horse's. Probably a little of each.

"Quit looking all over the place and memorize the route from the stable to Old Montreal," orders Alice, beside himself. "That's what I'm trying to show you!"

"How come you're so mean, Alice? I just want …"

"Out."

"What?"

"Get the hell out. You're getting on my nerves. You talk too much. Gives me an earache. Hurry up, get down! You don't want to see my ugly face when I'm mad."

Marie is alone in the middle of a deserted street in the Far Ouest. She has no idea where she is, but she's managed to get into Griffintown. She watches Alice and his no-name horse trotting away. Around her, a number of posters advertise that a man has disappeared.

✳ ✳ ✳

SITTING ON THE YELLOW buggy Poney is hitched to, John turns onto Ottawa Street, cursing the potholes. No driver wanted this calèche, which was reputed to be very unsteady: mustard yellow on a brown horse isn't very appealing. But John has never had trouble convincing tourists. He is less flamboyant than some of Halflinger's, but he inspires confidence.

He's glad to see Poney again after spending time with the dun-coloured horse the day before. He walked him around the Basilica, and the horse bolted at the slightest rustling of leaves on trees. John realized that horse wouldn't be spending the summer in Griffintown. As for Poney, he's a veteran, always walking at a good clip, straight ahead, calm but alert. John's not unhappy to see him again. From his seat in the calèche, he tells him so. Poney directs one ear towards where the voice comes from. The horse deciphers mercy towards him in John's tone.

Suddenly, a sound draws John's attention. The mysterious pink door of a shed he passes every day, always closed, half-opens. A girl comes out. Seeing him approach, she holds up her thumb. John recognizes the girl as the one he came across at the stable.

"Did Alice expel you already?"

"He's not very patient," Marie notes as she approaches John.

"What's in that shed, anyway?" asks John.

"I'll tell you if you let me spend the day with you."

"Never mind …"

"What's your problem? I'm trying to learn what to do…. With everything going on I don't even know where I am. This is a real no-man's land."

Clip, clip, clip, clop, clip, clip. The yellow calèche pulls away. Disheartened, out of ideas, Marie loosens her hair, lies down on the sun-warmed asphalt. The dust soils her hair. In a way, this is the first step in a long introduction: to become a calèche driver she must first let the grime and the filth settle on her like a second skin. The smell will follow.

Clip, clip, clop, clip — John is coming towards her with a mischievous smile.

"I was just killing time," he says.

"Ha! Ha! Very funny …"

"Don't look at me like that. Now, hop in before I change my mind."

"Your horse has a loose shoe," Marie points out as she steps into the calèche.

"I'm beginning to understand why Alice kicked you out."

"A hole."

"What?"

"There's a big hole on the other side of the pink door."

"What's in the hole?"

"Nothing. And it stinks to high heaven. Not as bad as the stable though."

John shows Marie how to wrap the reins around her fingers, neither absolutely English-style nor western, the idea being ultimately to learn to hold them in one hand without losing the proper tension in the reins, in a sliding U that seems complicated for a novice but comes naturally to an experienced coachman. Any rider recycled as a coachman finds it strange at first not to form one body with the horse, not to have her under him, not to be able to communicate with her through posture, seat, positioning of legs; this is all replaced by tone of voice, and its role is more decisive than might be thought. Marie knows the proper voice to use with horses: open, straightforward, slightly authoritarian, as if she were speaking to a troubled child, never telling a lie. Her true apprenticeship is beginning.

John teaches her how to slide the lunging whip between her fingers without losing the proper tension in the reins. She's against it, doesn't want to. "Take it anyway, to get rid of jerks that pass you too close to the calèches. There'll be some, you'll see." Marie learns how to sweep the horizon, near and far, with her gaze. The apprentice soaks up all of John's advice, drinks in all his knowledge of calèches, making the teacher generous and verbose in his teaching.

"When you get to know your horse you'll be able to do like Dédé." He goes on, "Dédé reads, sleeps, eats, and does Sudoku while driving Beauté. She's the calmest mare, but also the slowest one, in all of Griffintown — slow enough to put you to sleep. For now, though, what tells you your horse won't bolt because of a plain old plastic bag wrapped around her hoof or because she sees an Amphi-Bus coming? You don't know her, you don't know what she's got in her belly, so keep your eyes open. I warn you, your first summer with the calèche won't be a picnic, it's not a job like anything else. The girls will be on your back.... That's how it is here: the girls look after the girls, the guys take care of the guys. You have to earn your place; nothing will be handed to you. It's rough.

You seem to know horses a little, that will help, but it's not everything. You don't know how to back up or how to replace the elastic around a wheel — just hit a corner of the sidewalk and off it comes—and if you're a bit too much of a know-it-all, trust me, you won't last long around here."

"Where are the woman drivers?"

"Oh, they'll come to you, don't worry. You'll be meeting them soon," John replies with a half-smile.

"You scare me with your stories."

"It's risky, driving a calèche. Imagine if the buggy overturned ... or if your horse came unhitched. Ooooooh, mommy wouldn't like to see that, little lady!"

Being called "little lady" is the most reassuring thing that's happened to Marie since she first set foot in Griffintown.

"You'll see," John goes on. "Most of the others aren't altar boys."

"Speaking of colleagues, how does a scrawny tough guy like Alice get a woman's name?"

"Because he looks like Alice Cooper. Everybody sees that but you. You're the only one that hasn't noticed."

Besides imposing on him by being in his calèche, Marie smokes his cigarettes. She does all sorts of things that usually exasperate John, like asking endless questions; some of them, several, he doesn't know how to answer. She asks where the horses and drivers go after the busy season. He's never heard anyone ask that so openly. He orders her to be quiet for a few minutes, to listen to the silence. She talks anyway but now he doesn't listen; his attention falls on her hair — long, straight, dark, like a mane; a lock of it tickles his arm when she turns to look to the left.

In Marie's posture and in the length of her neck there's a reminder of the slender nobility and the bearing of fillies still warm from their mothers' flank, the ones that don't come to Griffintown. He dreams that Marie would sprain her wrists if her horse bolted and she tried to rein him in. This summer — his last — will be different from the others. It's written in the washed-out sky with its ochre glints. In Griffintown, the musky grime runs into the blue of the sky.

* * *

WITH PAUL GONE, ONE of the drivers or horsemen would have to take his turn as top man so the ring would keep moving. The question was on the lips of everybody in the Saloon. Who? Who could assume that vital role? Griffintown was now as vulnerable as a hen blown upside down by a violent gust. They'd have to get her back on her feet, fast.

Several candidates stand out: Georges, the star driver, a proud and reliable man but one who'd rather concentrate on his own concerns.

Evan has been Paul's assistant for a number of years. That more humble position is his by right. All eyes turn towards him.

Evan steps up. With his thirst for power and prestige, which he dwells on too much, he sounds suspicious. Brows are knit. His candidacy is struck off. Everyone knows his dark side and the shadow zone where he founders at times with no warning. His "bad spells," as he calls them. The leader has to be at all times solid and upright.

He hopes for more but he'll adapt. Besides, he has no choice. This coachmen's culture with its old-fashioned laws is all he has left.

When John opens the double doors, several see him as a candidate. They know he is loyal and fair, honest. But John turns down the offer, claiming this summer will be his last and that it's better for those remaining to look for someone who wants to put down roots in Griffintown. "The Indian?" suggests John. The Indian, a Huron-Wendat exiled to Montreal, chokes on his beer and wonders if they're pulling his leg. "No way," he replies. Anyway, he's busy enough with his small company that sells contraband cigarettes.

Lloyd relinquishes his video lottery terminal for two minutes and turns towards his co-workers.

"Billy?" he suggests.

"Not a bad idea," says John. "But his hands are full already."

"Le Rôdeur?" Georges suggests. "He was back at the stable a few days ago …"

"No, not him," says Joe, one of the seniors. "He's as deaf as a post. He misses parts of what people say, he disappears now and then …. If he was a horse he'd have been sent to the glue factory long ago."

✳ ✳ ✳

BILLY IS CLEANING OUT the stall when the phone in the stable rings. He puts down the shovel, wipes his forehead on his sleeve and answers. The exchange with John lasts several seconds, then the groom, annoyed, hangs up without saying goodbye. First, he hates to leave the stable, especially when there's no one around, which happens rarely — in fact never. Second, he still has work to do: finish the stalls, bring out the bags of sawdust, throw a few shovelfuls under the horses' hooves …. His day is far from over.

In the harness shed, on a plank nailed to the wall, an old western saddle has been hanging forever. Billy climbs up on the blacksmith's ladder and slides the object onto his forearm. A few drops of neat's-foot oil to nourish the leather wouldn't hurt but he doesn't have time. He runs a rag over the pommel and the cantle and appraises with a glance the length of the girth, much too short for a plow horse but the scraps of leather in the trunk will make an ideal extension.

Maggie. He wants to ride Maggie because her back is concave and her crupper is high. The mare lets herself be saddled up without budging, but when Billy tightens the girth she bites the air, emits two muted clacks with her yellow teeth. He has to climb the ladder to haul himself up to Maggie's back, seventeen hands high. Up there, the view is quite unlike the one from the driver's seat. The altitude is similar but the sensation is different. Rider and horse form one body, symbiosis becomes possible. The horse's energy, the pounding of her hooves on the ground reverberates all the way to the movements of the rider's backbone which rolls from the pelvis at the same rhythm. Continuity, proximity of bodies, meeting of leather and skin unshackled by wood, iron, metal, space.

Rider and steed march across the bridge, then trot to the Saloon. Billy knots the reins around the post, leads the mare to drink from the brass trough. She inhales slowly, eyes half-closed, and the long hairs of her fine beard dance in the water.

The groom waits until she's finished to push open the doors of the bar.

✳ ✳ ✳

THROUGH THE WINDOW THE drivers recognize Maggie's dappled croup, but mostly they notice the absence of a calèche behind her and nasty sores where the wooden traces have worn the hide of her thighs. Billy's silhouette stands out against the light, dust drifting there, motionless as the mist. Everything is silent as he passes; his heels ring out on the ceramic tiles. He sits down at the old guys' table, between Georges and Joe, who pours him a pint of horse piss.

It's been a long time since a man has arrived at the Saloon on horseback. Dan doesn't remember the last time. Paul's death, the council of drivers, and now a man on horseback: so many worrisome signs that prove the face of Griffintown has changed. The barman's hand is trembling; he turns to look at the head and shoulders of Boy, an unchanging figure, frozen in time, while the earth seems to disintegrate beneath his feet.

✳ ✳ ✳

The Founding Horse

It is said that before the first horse arrived, Griffintown was a ghost town, a dead place abandoned to its dust and rust, its ghosts. When the hooves of a draft animal sank into the beaten earth in the spring, everything changed.

A native of the Beauce, Boy had shoulders that were accustomed to farm labour. On his arrival in Griffintown, he was assigned to deliver ice and milk. In town, they recognized by their sound his hooves, which were fitted with iron shoes in winter, bare in summer. When children offered him lumps of sugar, Boy's grey lips would touch down cautiously on their palms and he would gobble the treat with one gloup. Small hands then made their way to his dark brown coat, gliding over his shoulder, stroking his side. The men got the idea one day to build a calèche for the pleasure of a ride in the countryside. They proceeded, respecting standards, to assemble it from carved wood, robust and embellished; it appeared quite delicate next to the more common big steel calèches.

After World War II, other horses joined Boy in Griffin-town, but the golden years of leisure and innocence were soon over. The changes occurred when the business became lucrative, as it became a front door for prohib-ited goods that passed through the port. In addition to powders and pills, furs, elephant tusks, and exotic birds that passed from hand-to-hand among the drivers who sometimes gave shelter under their seats to men on the run, there were illegal immigrants, ex-cons, and individuals sentenced to death. Everything could be bought. One day, a tiger was actually moved into a stall.

The Italian mafia didn't take long to get involved, imposing its will through barbaric methods. To shake up the man, the horse had to be targeted. Boy was stabbed in the night. He bled to death in the blood-red straw, aorta slashed, eyes riveted to the east. But the sun never rose. That was when a breach was opened that was never checked, a passage towards the gloom in which only Laura Despatie, Paul's mother, learned how to function. The fate of Griffintown and its dark ramifications had rested mainly in her hands ever since, and she mastered the situation fairly well. She was known as "La Mère." It had been a long time since she'd been seen prowling in the vicinity. When she turned up at the Saloon, it was in the drivers' interest to stand up straight and to display their best behaviour. It was her idea to stuff Boy and hang his head and shoulders on the wall of the Hôtel Saloon.

From his position, Boy could see everything, pick up complaints and confidences, know in detail the grandeur and the misery in the lives of the coachmen who always talked about themselves through their horses. And so, when Dédé complained about an old nag with a limp, he was actually talking about his hangover. And when Lloyd referred to his mare as a rotting carcass, it was his whole life he was cursing. His regrets, his depression, even his self-hatred were encapsulated in the word Charogne, the name he'd given his fast and slender racehorse who was the most precious thing he owned. From his perch, "Norm's first horse" — which appeared on the plaque — could sense the tenderness coiled within the insult.

✳ ✳ ✳

BILLY ACCEPTS HIS FATE as inevitable. One more weight on his shoulders, the last thing he needs, but he would rather take on that role than see the stable fall into the hands of someone like Evan. In any case the question has been settled; at least there's that. He accepts the cigarette the Indian offers, puts his cap back on, and bows to the coachmen. Maggie is still waiting for him, an unmoving block of splendour. Behind the ashy water of the canal and the scorched hills, the city spreads out — its skyscrapers, its hustle and bustle, an airplane in the sky, the explosion of promise for the new millennium, the modern life that is beating all around, roaring and crashing. None of that has come to the Far Ouest yet.

Billy lengthens the stirrup by seven or eight holes to give himself a step up. He mounts the horse and sees that a number of drivers, curious, have approached. Georges, Joe, the Indian, and Lloyd have watched him clamber up, perplexed but amused. They're outside the building, smoking, coughing, wrapped in the grime of Griffintown, their grey eyes, their tanned skin, their clothes in unrelieved sepia and their cowboy boots that tamp the sand and dust, four ragged crooks under his supervision. He leaves them promptly, squeezing Maggie's sides.

Billy crosses the boundaries to get to the next area in search of something to eat. He craves a burger and goes to the drive-through lane. Passersby look him over as if they've never in their lives met a horse, as if his mount had five feet. They observe him steadily. All of this gets on his nerves intensely.

Going back to Griffintown, he is overcome by a strange impression. Yet nothing has changed. The pink door, intact, still closed. Ugly scars crack the asphalt of the streets. The grocery cart has pride of place at the summit of a hill of metal debris. The first drifts of pollen dance on the street like lost souls; each choosing a side, depending on the mood of the wind. The missing-person notices on telephone poles all over are still in place. The ink is paler because of the dew and the paper is slightly swollen, but Paul on the steps of a church is recognizable at first glance, a smile showing all his teeth. Nothing has changed during Billy's brief absence, yet everything seems different. The echo of horseshoes on manhole covers rebounds off the door of a warehouse. The air has chilled as if a ghost has passed. Billy muses that he and his mare are alone in the world.

As he approaches the tin castle he hears hungry horses pawing the ground. Train time has come and gone; they're annoyed. He unsaddles his mount quickly, takes it into its stall, piles a bale of hay in the wheelbarrow, cuts the cord, and starts to feed the animals. A new horse he hasn't had time to name nips his shoulder, another has bloodshot eyes. He thinks that from now on and throughout the season, the drivers as well as the horses will depend on him. And he remembers, at the sight of a three-legged cat speeding by with a mouse in its mouth, that it's been a long time since he last filled its bowl. The fate of Griffintown weighs heavily on his shoulders.

When he has distributed all the rations of oats, Billy goes to the kitchen for a glass of water. That is when he sees on the table, standing unscathed, perfectly unharmed, Paul's second boot planted like an arrow. Billy clenches his jaws so hard he breaks a tooth.

THE CONQUEST

THANKS TO SKETCHES AND everyday tragedies, the heart of Griffintown beats again.

The new horses have had time to become familiar with the territory, its murmur, its traps, its exhalations, the voices of the drivers. Not many tenderfeet have found a mentor; three or four have persevered but only Marie is likely to stick it out until the end of summer. As for the drivers, they've hooked up again with a loved animal or broken in a new arrival, then repainted the corners of damaged fenders, oiled the leather of their harness, their boots and the uprights of the bridles, sanded the chipped wood of the shafts. Men and horses have done everything possible to get the season off to a good start, hooves agile and well shod. Even if the death of Paul Despatie haunts the drivers, they have to forge ahead and start stacking the hay — that's what Paul would have wanted. La Mouche has tightened his grip, flits around Lloyd and Gerry as if they were a display of meat. Foolishly planted on the skyline, the cross on Mont Royal is of no help to destitute coachmen.

When he's not flanked by his ward, John wanders as night falls, has a beer at the stable with Billy, new master of the house.

The latter now has his own horse, a world to keep turning and a dead man on his hands to be dealt with. "Every driver has a horse and a calèche," he repeats as if to reassure himself. But as soon as John leaves, the groom will sit cross-legged on the roof of his trailer, smoke a lot, think things over, spit into the dust. Billy works fiercely, relentlessly at assembling the pieces of an ambitious puzzle that is missing too many pieces.

The month of May passes, the torments are still there.

✻ ✻ ✻

IN OLD MONTREAL, AT the top of Place Jacques-Cartier, Le Rôdeur sits on his lawn chair, wears a mischievous smile: he has just robbed an American tourist who had the misfortune to lean over and ask for directions. And that's it! Gone, the wallet under his prominent belly. The spoils: a thick wad of US bills, some credit cards, and three passports, enough to pay for a steak, a bottle of Jack Daniel's, and some contraband cigarettes.

"What's that worth, an American passport?" he asks Joe. "No idea. Talk to La Mouche's guys in the Old Port. And bring me a coffee when you come back."

"Sure, boss!"

He tears down the hill on his bike, taking the small street perpendicular to the courthouse, then turns right and heads for the Alexandra Quay. Le Rôdeur meets John who is leading a new horse hitched to the yellow buggy. Marie holds the reins. The errand boy remembers that he heard some drivers gossiping about them. He also notices some tourists in the calèche. John must have picked them up when he got to the old city, not at the stand, which is disapproved of when the season is in full swing but acceptable for another week or two.

Seeing Le Rôdeur go by on his bike, John smiles, shouts, "Hey, champ!" to which the other man replies with a discreet nod. He hates being called that. The underlying irony wipes out the small amount of pride he still has left. He turns into an alley of damp cobblestones, cursing the coachman.

Le Rôdeur

Legend has it that Le Rôdeur stopped washing three decades ago. For a long time he hasn't scratched himself and is protected now by a fine patina of grime. Over the years he's been nicknamed "The Vagrant." He's become insensitive to cool nights spent in a stall in the stable until the end of October, under the bridges in November, and God only knows where in the winter. When he opens his mouth two gold teeth gleam in the centre of a row of stubs blackened by contraband tobacco. That's all he owns. Le Rôdeur, like Alice, Lloyd, and several others, has his moments of distress and distraction. He disappears for a few days after dropping in on Evan in his trailer, then comes home, face drawn and wearing the jacket he's stolen from a highway employee, inside out.

"Le Rôdeur's got his head up his ass," declared Billy, and the errand boy went to the stand but refused to help anyone.

If Le Rôdeur was evasive when one night John ventured to ask some questions about his past, it was simply because he devoted himself with all his might, all his life, to forgetting it by exhausting himself with whatever came to hand, nose, or veins.

An orphan who suffered at the hands of a state-run Catholic orphanage, Le Rôdeur spent his youth in a psychiatric institution. For a while he sought refuge in madness, but it rejected him. He escaped from the asylum through a window, in the middle of the night, after a sexual assault. Like Evan, Le Rôdeur escaped from an institution that had nearly wiped him out. Both were damaged by their past but they were survivors, noble in their own way for having survived. They moved forward in life as if tracing the Stations of the Cross, overwhelmed yet struggling.

Le Rôdeur lived in the stable for a good ten years, in the stall reserved for him by Billy and Paul. In winter, when the horses' breath was no longer enough to warm his hands, he could sometimes be seen seeking a little warmth in the entries of Métro stations or begging around Square Viger. Because he had lost confidence in the world, Le Rôdeur had adopted anonymity — not having an official or social identity suited him. It was a camouflage and until proven otherwise, no one had been able to track him down. He lived like a partridge with fawn-coloured plumage, pecking his substance in the fallen leaves; he melted into his environment.

✳ ✳ ✳

LE RÔDEUR'S ABRUPT TURN and the shadow of a bicycle projected in front of Poney make him speed up. Marie pulls moderately on the reins and reassures the horse. Concentrating and in a state of alert, she has gained a great deal of self-confidence over the past weeks. John decides this will be Marie's last day of training. He'll notify Billy that evening.

Le Rôdeur walks past the stand with Joe's coffee. John beckons him to come closer. He puts the money for three coffees in Le Rôdeur's hand. "Keep one for yourself."

"You're generous," observes Marie.

"Not really. It's to be sure of good service when I ask him to get me my dinner. You'll see, nothing here is free. Each person does his own business and the balance is maintained, like an ecosystem, which is why I said 'No' when you asked if I wanted you to get me something to drink. Fill the boiler with water for Poney if you want to be useful."

The water is much cooler than in the stable. Poney laps slowly, then crunches the lump of sugar offered by his new partner-in-crime. Marie scratches him under the leather harness, at the level of the withers. He bends his head and gently paws the ground with his right front hoof, hopes she'll scratch his whole body like that — and she will at the stable later on, with a curry comb, when she unhitches him. On the way back, John repeats his advice one last time: "Talk about Indians to Europeans, architecture and history to Americans, point out costume stores to families, and remind the few Montrealers who'll climb on board of the significance of Je me souviens. Take sections of lanes when it's too congested elsewhere, as much as possible avoid the cobblestone rue Saint-Paul — it wrecks hooves — be careful you don't get stuck at a red light on the Bonaventure hill and if it's about to happen, go at a trot or even a gallop, spare your horse. The stands in front of the Basilica and at the bottom of Place Jacques-Cartier are the territory of the experienced drivers; until you know how to back up, avoid them and keep a low profile. If a tourist gets on your nerves, make him get out, exactly like Alice did with you. Remember there's just one master on a calèche: the driver. Watch out for trucks carrying a revolving barrel of cement; some horses, sure that the barrel is going to roll over them, will bolt when the trucks come their way. Don't put your cash in the rear trunk when Le Rôdeur is guarding your calèche, and when you're trying to attract tourists the action happens between your horse's nose and the trunk of the calèche. Stay within the limits of your territory — like a hooker. Stay away from La Mouche. At any rate, you aren't the kind of girl who borrows cash from a loan shark…. Change your horse's diaper as soon as there's manure in it, otherwise you'll have flies and the drivers will lash out at you. To say nothing about the local residents who hate us nearly as much as taxi drivers. Your place here, you have to earn it. You don't have to report to Billy. If his calèche and his horse come back intact, if you manage to get some customers into your calèche and bring money back to the stable, he'll leave you alone. It's the drivers that rule the place among themselves. In other words, if you don't work out, you'll know pretty fast. One last thing: at the end of the day keep your whip nearby, like I taught you. A driver comes back to the stable with full pockets, word gets around."

Marie watches John's lips, lips that say important things she won't hear again except in the background. They don't belong to the same world. John is a good ten years older than she is, but something about him intrigues her. It must be the mentor's self-confidence, his manners, at once gruff and tender, the heat, the leather, the air dusted with gold and the mirages breathed in Griffintown. John, who initially didn't want to coach the new driver, is surprised to find himself trying to protect Marie, to be afraid for her. She's pretty, that's obvious. Desirable, even, but too young, too lovely, too shrewd for him. He's a cowboy, a man who dislodges wood shavings from between his toes every night when he takes off his socks. At the end of summer, or before, the girl will go back to her world about which he knows nothing, she won't last long in Griffintown; her time in the Far Ouest is probably just a passing fancy. And there's something childish about her that sets his teeth on edge. Marie spends her time bumming smokes from him and asking uncalled-for questions: Why does Evan have tears tattooed on his cheeks? Why did you leave the halter under Poney's bridle? What ratio of oats in his feed? What language does Lloyd speak? She doesn't know about Paul Despatie or she wouldn't have left him for a second. At the end of the day John can't wait for her to get back on her bike and take off so he can admire her ass, then finally have some peace. And the worst is that in the evening when he sits at a table in the Saloon over a glass of horse piss, his thoughts fly away to Marie.

Soon, though, all that will be over. She'll learn to fly with her own wings, they'll occupy different stands. She will go to the top of Place Jacques-Cartier with the new drivers, he to the very bottom with the regular visitors; they will meet now and then, by chance, say "Hello" .... John hopes she knows how to sort things out, but when he sees her tighten recklessly the reins between her knees long enough to fix her chignon when her horse is still moving, he doubts it.

Going back to the stable, Poney raises his upper lip and emits a brief, shrill whinny by way of a greeting to Marilyn, a new mare Joe has just unhitched. When Poney senses a female presence in the stable, he's immediately drawn by her exciting scent that stands out in the mustiness. He would like to be next to her in the line of stalls, but Rambo has slipped in between them. That bothers Poney so much that he kicks the stretch of wall separating him from his neighbour. He flattens his ears, then regains his self-control; he'll have all summer to be close to her, to get drunk on her enticing secretions. Marilyn is standing unharnessed, covered with lather, incredibly blond. When he passes behind the mare, Poney makes the most of it to inhale the flower between her hindquarters.

* * *

AFTER UNHITCHING HER HORSE, Marie gets on her bike and rides away from the tin castle, smiling when she thinks of the look on Poney's face and on Rambo's and Marilyn's when they see the treat she's prepared for them in the stall: on a cube of hay she had set sections of apple and chunks of a big crisp carrot, a dozen pink peppermints, tossed a handful of oats and mixed in some good, sticky molasses.

Heading east, she drives past the old city to watch the evening coachmen she doesn't know so well. In front of the Basilica one of them, decked out in a derby hat and the kind of glasses with a mesh design made famous by Kanye West a few years ago, is hitched to a light caleche and a race horse wearing a top hat and dark glasses too.

Alice is there, looking for something, a light for his cigarette probably. A driver holds out a lighter; he seems calmer now. Then a horse attracts Marie's attention: thickset, with the proportions of a small buffalo; an incredible coat, between maiden's blush rose and butterscotch macaroon, a speckled vacillation that spreads to his whole body; his nostrils and mouth are white, a detail that cracks her up; she stops for a moment to touch him.

Past Berri Street, real, predictable, odourless. Crossing the border at the east she feels as if she's falling off a cliff. In her head still dances the memory of the unusual horse she just met. The details of her new life as a calèche driver fill her thoughts: the carton of molasses that leaked all over her backpack; her bicycle tires that need air; the examination on driving the calèche that's coming soon; John's voice when he lavishes advice. John, whom she is anxious not to let down. Outside the limits of Griffintown, time seems to have stopped.

✳ ✳ ✳

CHAMPION WAS THE COMPANION of Mignonne, an immaculate, mythical Pegasus who watches over the horses and haunts Alice still. The old gelding, one of the few horses in the stable to have trotted in the city during the Golden Age of the calèche, is starting on what will probably be his last season. For two or three years now, he has been shuffling his feet, which the experienced drivers can't stand. At the very least, Champion must be allowed twenty minutes more than any other horse to get to the tourist area. At times Paul comes in the pickup truck to take him back to the stand and spare both the animal's and the driver's patience. He has to be spared and that's why Billy has decided that Champion will spend the summer being crammed with apples by Marie, like a doting grandpa entrusted to the care of a pretty nurse.

Reserved for veterans like Champion is the box stall at the very back of the aisle, with a window looking out on the stream, a lot more spacious and airy than the usual stall. It is the greatest privilege granted to the old horses.

* * *

"COME HERE," SAYS BILLY to Marie, leading her to the box stall. "There's a horse I want you to meet."

She inspects Champion closely, gliding her hand over the horse to study his temperament and let him smell her. Some bruising on the withers; old scars on the croup (Marie knows what salve to use to restore smooth hair to the man-handled hide), some swelling in the right forefoot that nothing but a good hydrotherapy session will reduce, then she'll see if he needs to be bandaged; the hair at the top of the tangled tail (did he get his worm powder last spring?); the drab coat, probably the accumulation of all that dust. She gives him a long shower and the grey water delivers a handsome, gilded chestnut creature that Marie dries gently. She untangles his mane, drips a bit of shampoo onto his tail, slowly massages his oversize shoulder, braids his hair, then ties onto several locks a flower of butter-and-eggs. The final touch: Vaseline to soften the gelding's chapped lips.

"Is that Champion?" asks Billy, incredulous, as he trundles past her with a wheelbarrow full of soiled straw.

He knows he's made the right decision. Marie is giving herself a treat and the old horse will be pampered all summer.

The person who keeps the tin castle going has to find the best combination of horse-driver-calèche, a puzzle that is complex and sometimes risky. Billy gazes now at the small wooden calèche, the oldest one, which is light and painted black.

"Get ready, Kid. We're going to hitch up Champion and that'll be your examination."

"For the permit, right away like that? Do you evaluate me?"

"You got it. That's how we do things here."

Tracing figure eights by zigzagging between two traffic cones for five minutes without hitting them, on a deserted blind alley not far from a sticky stream, and that's the driving exam.

* * *

SITTING IN THE LICENCE bureau office, Marie smiles as she thinks about the evaluation, which turned out to be much less arduous than expected. That the world of calèches, about which she sometimes wonders if she is dreaming, intersects with an institution, more specifically government buildings, amuses her. The smell of her soiled boots repels those sitting around her, tangible proof that it's all very real. Marie celebrates privately the marriage of two worlds she would have thought irreconcilable. She has seen horses in the city. A small victory, an exploit, a rapture.

After she obtains the precious document and hangs it proudly around her neck; the confirmed driver gets back on her bike and repeats the trip, this time to the Far Ouest. John said there was one last stage in her training as a driver — a detail, but an important one. After that, she will be able to start the season knowing all there is to know about the profession. Marie hopes it's not an initiation. She hopes with all her might that she won't be asked to drink stagnant water from the canal. The bubbles that come up slowly from the depths leave her perplexed.

She drops her bike to the ground not even bothering to lock it. Her mind elsewhere, Marie goes into the calèche garage. Two well-behaved black horses are waiting to be harnessed but John isn't there. Joe appears with his usual dumb look; he has big pliers to take God knows what from God knows whom. She nods at him without expecting anything in return, then heads for the stable. John and Billy are in the alley, arguing about a situation that's bothering them. They are talking sotto voce; she pricks up her ear and notes that John has lost his usual composure.

"It doesn't make sense, Bill. For weeks now he's been in the cold. Paul deserves better than that. We have to get him out of there!"

"And put him where?"

The new driver understands that with horsemen, explanations don't come when you want them; you have to advance patiently in the dark. Marie has also noticed that when she stops asking, the replies come by themselves.

"Okay," he says. "Let's go."

She doesn't bother asking where, but is still surprised that they go on foot, taking neither horse nor calèche.

Getting down from their drivers' bench, John and Marie are exposed and much more vulnerable.

They sweep into the damp night of Griffintown.

✳ ✳ ✳

AT THE HÔTEL SALOON, Joe sits by himself at the bar. Lloyd plays video poker. Three coachmen sip beer. The regulars, including Gerry, who drives the spotted horse at the Basilica, stand. Alice seems to have snorted, swallowed, or smoked something too strong. He goes to the men's room every fifteen minutes, cursing. Some local patrons complete the tableau, around twenty people in all. A minor commotion is set off by the entrance of Marie and John. The old drivers are torn between happiness at the sight of a female and irritation generated by the arrival of a neophyte among them. John has warned Marie: "Act like nothing's going on. They'll balk at first, but they'll get used to it." Advice that she quickly ignores. "Hey, guys," she says when gazes turn in her direction. "I've got my permit." A reaction so unexpected and contrary to their usual behaviour that the drivers don't know how to behave. Behind the bar, Dan drops his dishcloth so he can follow the scene.

"You make me hot," John whispers in Marie's ear.

"I beg your pardon?!"

John immediately regrets his choice of words and tries to regain his composure.

"I told you to keep a low profile ... but don't worry, they look like they think you're cute. You've got guts and charisma and they'll help when it's time to take on clients."

Dan arrives with two drafts.

"Horse piss, on the house," he announces. "No charge for the little lady."

The alcohol moistens palates, washes thoughts, dissolves acid, and sweetens dispositions. At the Hôtel Saloon tonight they'll drown all sorts of things: the death of Paul, the fact that his murderer is still on the loose, the stress of the past few weeks, the apprehension that goes along with the beginning of the season, the weight of accumulated debts, the grip of the loan shark, the impression of being alone and tough, regret at having let his luck go by too long ago for any hope of bringing it back .... Unburdened, the drivers are transformed into characters larger than life. It's at these moments that they most embody their legend. All under Boy's feeble eyes, a pitiless reminder of the day to come.

Marie has the smart idea of buying a round for the drivers. Their brotherhood, which seemed impenetrable a month before, is now offering her a hand. She has left the periphery. She knows now that she is one of them. She stops at the mounted head and shoulders of Boy and imagines him patrolling the streets of Griffintown.

"Back then, calèches weren't used for carting fat Americans who're sick of having to drag themselves around. The horses delivered things," Dan explained.

"I see. Were they happier back then?"

"That I couldn't say, but they were useful, even necessary, not just decorative."

"What did that horse die of?" she asked, intrigued.

"Bled to death after a wild man took a knife and slashed his chest." Marie's thoughts become confused and muddled, she feels the ground slip away under her boots, the drivers' words slacken off. She faints.

* * *

WHEN MARIE COMES TO, John is bending over her, talking gently but firmly, in the tone he uses to soothe horses. He suggests calling a taxi but once she's recovered, Marie goes to the stable to make sure Champion has everything he needs. Tomorrow will be her first day as a driver and she wants her horse to be in good shape.

In his stall, Champion, exhausted, is lying on his side, sleeping so soundly he's snoring. Marie pictures him as a colt, a tiny creature with downy hair taking refuge in the flank of his enormous Belgian mother with an engorged udder. It is when the horses lie on the ground to listen to the secrets imprisoned in the earth that Marie catches a glimpse of what they were before they washed up in Griffintown.

Taking advantage of John's momentary inattention while he is in the garage rummaging for matches under his driver's bench, Marie goes out to get a cube of hay so there will be sustenance for Champion when he wakes up. She knows more or less where the bullets are stored but here in the dark, she can't see much. She spots a door at the back of the stall in the corridor, holds her hand out to open it, touches something warm: a hand.

"Who's there?" barks a man's voice.

Taking refuge in the shack where he sleeps on a chair with one eye open, Le Rôdeur flicks his lighter to see who has the nerve to disturb his sleep.

"Oh!" says Marie, stunned. "I didn't know that you .... What are you doing?"

"Sleeping, for Christ's sake, haven't you got eyes in your head? Shut the door and get the hell out."

Going back to the stable, she inhales the moist, familiar breath of the animals. Hearing the horses inhale, and smelling the sweet aroma they exude in sleep, the fine, scarcely visible perspiration, like dew — this comforts her. She likes the presence of the sleeping horses. In the garage, Marie notices a man on the floor, dozing on cushions: a driver she doesn't know. John isn't around, she finds it strange that he has abandoned her in the middle of the night. It's getting late; dawn will soon be there. Marie takes her bike out of the prickly bushes and approaches the broken edge of the sidewalk as a rider nears an obstacle, an impulse she has never shed. Suddenly she hears her name called, then the footsteps of a man making his way towards her in the night. Marie recognizes John's silhouette. "I thought you'd gone away and left me behind!"

"Griffintown's dangerous at this time of night," says John. "I'll see you home." Dawn, complicit, sheds its milky light in front of them, guiding their footsteps. In the old city, not a living soul. They follow the Lachine Canal and rue de la Commune, then John leaves Marie at the border of the territory. She gives him an enigmatic smile then gets back on her bike and speeds down the bicycle path on Berri. The cowboy with time on his hands, without a mount, stands for a long moment, unmoving, as he watches Marie disappear, then takes off again for the ghost town whose streets at this hour are paced by the silent hooves of horses made of mist.

* * *

ALREADY DAWN. STRETCHED OUT on the flowered eiderdown on a narrow pallet in his trailer, Billy can't get back to sleep. He stands up, pulls on jeans and a shirt, climbs onto his bed, and takes down the crucifix Paul Despatie acquired when he bought the trailer. He goes out and tosses it into the syrupy water of the stream, then comes back to make coffee. On the dented trailer wall remains the persistent ghost of a pale cross. And on the small mat at the door, Paul's boots — the one found in the water and the second, placed on the kitchen table by an intrusive visitor. Billy considers them at length, then turns to his mother's picture and finally, the clock. Nearly five a.m.. La Grande Folle won't be long.

There's no one here who knows how the old transsexual hooker ended up in Griffintown. No matter, she's part of the landscape now and has been for seven years. La Grande Folle arrives to clean the calèches when the rooster crows, which suits everyone. She returns every year, looking five years older, reliably appearing at the beginning of June when the season takes off and a rumour of abundance still floats in the balmy air. When she leaves the stable at dawn, vulnerable and weary, La Grande Folle can't distinguish between bats and hummingbirds. The groom can't get back to sleep after the incident with the crucifix. The investigation isn't progressing; Billy moves at a snail's pace, stamping on the roof of his trailer, obsessed with Paul's body, twisted and frozen. And now he wants to go on horseback. Half-past five a.m.: the one moment of the day when horses and drivers leave him alone. Billy's gaze lights on the horizon. Then he does something inexplicable: he dons the boots of Paul Despatie and heads for the stable.

He strokes the flank of his mare while she finishes her ration of oats, then saddles her and leads her through the sleeping streets to see how the new shoes fit. In spite of the early hour, the mare ought to be full of beans, but she stays placid and calm, respectful of the character of his race. He looks up at the direction of the clouds: soft streaks of mist on a sky that ranges from pastel to lead. The light is coming from the south-east, as if it takes its vigour from the fluorescent lighting in the Costco warehouse and is born from a part of the city Billy knows all too well.

✳ ✳ ✳

The Last of the Irish

Legend has it that beneath the department store survived the traces of an old Irish village razed in 1964, the year of his birth. Billy knows by heart the tales of bad luck, memories of potatoes and stewed pigeons that are stirred by this part of town.

A few years ago several Irishmen were driving calèches. Then Scott moved to the States, Andrew was behind bars, Jimmy became a trucker, and Leo Leonard sold off his last horses. Until very recently, once a season, generally in August when it was hot and they were on edge, Scott, Andrew, Jimmy, and Billy himself would hitch up a horse and go down to Goose Village to meditate in their own way at the foot of the black stone not far from the Victoria Bridge. Billy hasn't set foot there for two or three years. Ever since his compatriots disappeared and he was condemned to bear by himself, at arm's length, the weight of his origins.

At Windmill Point, not far from the old train station, four or five thousand Irish were put in quarantine in the mid-nineteenth century because of a typhus epidemic.

On her death bed, his mother Jane made him promise

to honour his ancestors, ghosts smothered beneath the asphalt of a parking lot built on the single grave where all the victims of typhus had been thrown. For the last Irishman in Goose Village, that impoverished heritage had become too great a liability.

Everything Irish that remains could be boiled down to a white plank decorated with clover brought home from a St. Patrick's Day party and nailed up in the stable to keep Champion's stall from caving in. There is also, hanging in the trailer, an old black-and-white photo of Jane, a serious look on her face. Towards the end, Jane no longer believed in anything and, knowing her days were numbered, asked her son to take down all the crosses in the house and burn them. She insisted on being buried out of the way under just a stone with no epitaph, anonymous, reflecting on how she had lived all those years. "I'm a simple passenger," she whispered in the ear of Billy, who was already fatherless. Those were her last words, dictated in a way that was hard to decipher. Billy was sixteen.

✳ ✳ ✳

THE LAST IRISHMAN REGRETS going back to Goose Village. While he is listening to his ancestors whisper in his ear that he must pay them a tribute, two vultures have crossed the limits of Griffintown. The men in black suits care nothing for their immediate environment. Backs to the stable, facing a wall of corrugated tin, they are debating, waving their arms in a way that suggests high-rise construction, the placement of something on a vast open space. Their self-assurance, their predatory smiles, and their Mercedes parked nearby suggest that generally these two men go where they want, quickly and in a straight line, that they belong to a race that generally doesn't come to Griffintown.

After a vigorous handshake, the Men from the City go back to their vehicle and drive away.

Someone has emptied the bottle of vodka he keeps in the refrigerator freezer. That's all Billy notices on his return. A hesitant light suddenly brightens his tangled thoughts. He has a hunch: Evan. It can only be him. Because of the vodka. And Paul. He has a duplicate of the keys to the boss's truck, thinks Billy, who doesn't know very well where that trail leads. Ever since he came home from Afghanistan, Evan hasn't been the same.

* * *

The Man Who Met a Windigo

In a time not so long ago, during the nineteen-eighties when things were going well for Paul and the coachmen came back to the stable every night with at least three or four hundred bells, even on weekdays, Evan had assumed the expression of the star-coachman long before Georges Prince. He had a movie star's looks and plenty of sex appeal. Business was going briskly for Paul, who at the time trusted him with his best horses. Evan had fallen in love with Kim, former dancer and twenty-five-cent hooker, who still worked the street when the day's returns hadn't been hefty enough for his liking. A glorious girl, with whom Evan had a son. The boy's birth sounded the end of what had been a wild party that had been

Evan's life since he'd started to drink at age of nine.

He decided to get a grip on himself, put back some order in his life, but there wasn't much on the horizon for a marginal type like him. Evan wanted to act quickly; he signed up with the Canadian Forces. He and Kim took a break from the world of the calèche for several years. She never came back to Griffintown. He limped there, face drawn, stooped, confused, too battered and bruised to go back to being a coachman but too proud to work as a groom. To anyone who dared to ask what had happened during the years when he was away, Evan would reply, staring into space, that he'd bumped into a Windigo in the desert and didn't want to talk about it.

And so he became Paul's assistant, the one who led the horses back to the stable in the semi-trailer and who at the end of every summer took responsibility for leading them to the place where they'd be made into glue, the one who drowned cats in the stream, the one who wept eternally tears of black ink. Ever since he'd met the Windigo, Evan's hands were stained with blood and his face tattooed with tears.

One day when he was drunk, he talked to Paul about the war in Afghanistan. He confessed that in the company of some infantrymen, he'd played football in a field with the head of a dead peasant and that at the time it had been good for him, even made him laugh. Afterwards, he was a changed man. He avoided telling Paul that he'd killed civilians and children, raped a woman as ordered by the Windigo. That was the story he'd poured out to the lieutenant. He was demobilized and came back to Griffintown. Within a short time, Evan's trailer was transformed into a crack house and that was the beginning of the end for several of the horsemen who thought they'd triumphed over their former vices. Every morning when she came to sluice down the calèches, La Grande Folle brought something in her purse to supply Evan's business. Most of the coachmen who succumbed managed to get over it, but some — like Billy's best friend, Ray — didn't have the strength. It was powerfully tempting and above all, it was right there, two steps away. It was enough to hold out an arm, to not look away, to say "I do" and swipe a few bills from the envelope to take up again with all that electricity and feel on his forehead the great black wing of indulgence. Every summer, like a weed that can't be uprooted. The person who comes face-to-face with the Windigo comes back to sow chaos, taking in his fall the vulnerable souls.

* * *

BILLY NOW CONSIDERS EVAN to be his prime suspect. In fact, a few days have passed since he last ran into him. At first he concluded that now with Paul gone, the little helper's jobs were rarer. Perhaps Evan had realized it would be of no use for him to stay behind and he too decided to get up and go. The groom is very happy no longer having to live under the same roof as Evan, no longer to tolerate his bad vibes and his trailer, but this complicates his access to the horses' shower.

Ever since he came home from Afghanistan, Evan has lost his ability to feel empathy, first for animals, then for his fellow creatures. The former coachman acts as if life owes him a living; he cultivates discord and resentment as others would a fertile field. He has always been thirsty for power — pondered, dissatisfied, irascible — following Paul, expecting a little of his boss's power to rub off on him. If he were a horse, it would have been said about him that he didn't have a good eye. He could have, in a megalomaniacal frenzy, eliminated the boss in order to take his place. Yes, it's a possibility, Billy concludes.

And that's when he catches sight of Ray, or rather his ghost, where he used to find the man himself at times, sitting on his beam in the calèche garage, legs dangling, feet without boots. Ray doesn't smile. His gaze, deep as a chasm, beams a hypnotic light that oddly soothes him. After all, Evan has at least one death on his conscience.

✳ ✳ ✳

Ray the Hanged Man

One evening — it must have been four years ago, long after the coachmen had gone out for the evening shift — Ray had forced the small cashbox, breeched the trap door with a hoof pick and a scraper so he could plunge his arm in to retrieve envelopes stuffed with money intended for Paul. A one-night junkie, Ray had unsealed them all to prolong his euphoria, stronger than his will. At dawn when there were no envelopes left, he felt that he'd never been so lucid, that he finally understood the smooth running of the world, his own in particular, which was proceeding crookedly, stumbling as it receded. He had a clear sense that there would be no way out, that it would be impossible to pay back the contents of the envelopes. And as he no longer had the strength to resist, to run away or to fight, Ray decided that the time was right to be done with it.

As he did every morning, Billy entered the stable through the calèche garage. He remembered as though it had happened just the day before: the big motionless body hanging at the end of a rope and his cowboy boots fallen to the floor. He'd had his friend's body taken down, put his boots back on and had wrapped him like a feverish baby in one of those woollen blankets full of bugs the coachmen stow in the trunk of the calèche in anticipation of the cooler late-season evenings. In time, the stable became a minefield of memories: the beam where Ray hanged himself; Mignonne's old min; a colleague's hat found in a locker after many years; dog-eared ancient photos in the harness shed; the name of an old horse jotted on a cigarette paper found at the bottom of a chest; the scratches on a calèche painted red that allow one to glimpse that it had once been brown. The memory comes alive again of a summer when it rained a lot.... In Griffintown, ghosts are at large, more of them than angels.

I N A DOWNTOWN SKYSCRAPER built on the fringes of the Far Ouest, the Men from the City meet around a model of Project Griffintown 2.0. On the stable's site where currently thistles, butter-and-eggs flowers, and clover are tangled together as in an English garden, will stand a conglomeration of luxury urban chalets with a view of the Lachine Canal.

This red-brick complex will be extended by several small units planted where now stands the tin castle on a carpet of loose stones — lair of the three-legged cat and an accumulation of the little bones of the birds he has devoured — near Billy's trailer. On the graves of Ray and Mignonne, the idea is to build a pharmacy, a gourmet food shop, and a parlour-boutique specializing in tea. In the murky stream where Paul and dozens of kittens have been swallowed up, clear water the colour of mirrors will flow. On the surface of the model, water lilies float and, with a little imagination, one can see them rippling gently under a favourable breeze.

The Men from the City have big plans for the neighbourhood. They see a village to populate, a territory to conquer and occupy. The Metro will have to extend to Griffintown so that new merchants will want to set up there. Coachmen, horses, and putrid fumes aren't part of the plan or the setting. What they want is for the grimy cowboys to surrender. In any case they belong to a bygone age and will have to withdraw. If not, other measures will be considered.

A T THE CORNER OF Murray and Ottawa streets, in what used to be Leo Leonard's Horse Palace where, until very recently, there were other draft animals, a little ball of foliage has formed around an uprooted root of clover. Rolling around made it eventually cling to whatever happened to be there, friable and light: clumps of old yellow grass; dried flower buds and forked horsehair; powdered horn; even a little marrow tangled in the grey sand with dandelion rootlets; veins of leaves from autumns past; seeds of sainfoin; bits of string and rough cord; pollen and crumbling iron; sparrow's fluff. The ball expands, more and more puffy and bulbous, twirls along the asphalt in the direction of rue des Seigneurs like a small soul in danger of panic.

* * *

ON THE WALL OF a warehouse, Marie observes the shadow cast by her calèche. Her posture and reflexes, those of a former rider, are still intact: back perfectly straight, focussed on destination; the proper tension in the reins; fully invested in communicating hand-reins-mouth with the animal. But after a minute or two of this system she realizes how ridiculous the system is. Champion knows the road much better that she does. Back stiff, smile feigned, none of that is necessary. In any case, so early in the morning, this sector of the Far Ouest is deserted. It's not an equestrian contest; there is no judge to please. East of McGill Street, the Far Ouest ends and the heart of downtown begins. In this neighbourhood the sky is no longer a faded blue as it is in Griffintown, but greyish-mauve because of the summer smog.

As soon as the light turns green, Champion resumes his pacing, not concerned in the least about the traffic, onto the busy thoroughfare and as far as Notre-Dame. There, things intensify for both driver and old horse. In one lane, there is a truck and some city employees. In the second, a large metal plate covers the pothole that city workers are getting ready to fill. Marie considers turning around, but they wave her on. Then she directs Champion to the plate. She has no choice: to get to the stand, they have to walk on it.

As soon as he senses the metal of his shoe touch the metal on the ground, Champion takes fright and starts to gallop, heading eastward at full tilt. Along the way, the wing of the calèche scratches several cars parked on the north side of rue Notre-Dame and with the speed, the elastics around the tires of the calèche give way. Marie tries in vain to rein in the horse, but Champion comes to a halt on his own a few metres farther, across from the Basilica and in front of some stunned onlookers. The horse's heart and Marie's are beating, two overworked pumps.

Marie jumps out and examines a gasping, breathless Champion, his nostrils dilated. She runs a hesitant hand along the

animal's flank, murmuring gently, along his thigh to the hock.
There are no visible injuries on his body, fortunately. Marie
fills a cauldron with water and while Champion laps greedily,
she calls Billy to give him the bad news, thinking this is her
first day as a driver and probably her last. She hasn't taken
on a single customer and she'll be obliged to hand over the
reins to someone else. She remembers hearing John and
several other drivers curse the project. Construction and
rain: two scourges. Marie doesn't really understand what has
happened. The old nag that's supposed to be the best friend
of all novice drivers, the Belgian said to be so calm and unflappable, bolted the first chance he got.

She's mad at Champion, the veteran, for shaking off his
lethargy without warning, mad at the city employees and
the winter that creates such holes in the streets, mad at John
and at Billy for not warning her of the danger, mad at
Le Rôdeur who'd mocked her by demanding five dollars to
keep an eye on her horse while she went to pick up the tire
elastic farther along Notre-Dame. Her years of riding, every
summer of her teenage years spent on horseback, are of no
use at all on a calèche. Marie is mad at herself for having
been convinced of the opposite. More than anything, she's
mad at herself for being so naive. She looks at her hand and
realizes she is shaking. Suddenly, Marie has doubts.

She realizes she has a grenade in her hand. It's dangerous
work, John told her so again and again and now she understands what he meant. She would have been able to catch the
animal if she'd been on his back, been able to control him by
the position of her legs and seat, by holding the reins tighter.
But when you're behind, it complicates everything. She recalls

the unbelievable story a driver, Joe, told her about the time years before when his horse, hitched to a calèche, jumped over a BMW. Marie didn't want to know how the story ended. Besides, she knows the drivers' tendency to exaggerate is strong. Marie thinks about John, who has spent several weeks showing her the ropes. At the end of the line the telephone rings and rings. Finally, Billy answers. "Billy, get over here, there's a problem." Fifteen minutes later, she spots him in the distance, riding Maggie, who comes along at a trot.

Billy makes a face at the sight of the line of damaged cars and realizes, as he leads his mount onto the metal plate, what has happened. Le Rôdeur comes running to join him.

"The Kid treated herself to quite a ride!"

"Hell of a kid, that Kid!" says Billy.

"I know. Fire me. I'll understand."

Billy goes to Champion and examines him. In a state of shock but no obvious injuries. The groom rubs his forehead, seems discouraged.

"It's not your fault," he declares. "Champion's got a phobia about those plates. He just has to put one foot on metal and as soon as he feels himself skating a little, soon as it goes skree, skree, the animal goes nuts. I forgot to tell you, you couldn't know."

Billy stretches the elastics around the tires and sends Marie to the stable, showing her a route with no metal plates.

"That's it for today. But you'll come back tomorrow as planned."

Billy slips business cards under the windshield wipers of cars with scraped sides, notes the licence numbers, and returns to Griffintown. There's no one to guard the tin castle and that worries him. On the way home he notices that the rain and the sun, the wind and the passing of time have nearly erased his missing person notices still stapled to the posts.

Knowing he'll get there long before Marie, he allows himself a little detour near the construction site behind the Horse Palace. In the midst of the scaffolding, Leo Leonard's stable is resisting as best it can, like something being tossed about by a storm, though it is encircled by hills of loose stones and brick. The old Irishman put it up for sale some years ago after he got rid of his last horses, but he's asking so much it's still on the market, being courted only by a heritage support group.

A few strides away, Billy notices they've started putting up condos. To get there, he takes a shortcut across an abandoned parking lot. And that's when he sees Paul's truck — what's left of it. Black, burnt, covered with graffiti. The windows are shattered. Billy slides his finger along the car body. Soot, dry and chalky. In the back of the truck the last of the Irish recognizes the crate of broken bits Paul took with him when he left. He gives the door a powerful kick. He lets out a howl like a coyote abandoned by its pack. His horse takes three steps to the side.

* * *

LATE THAT AFTERNOON, WHEN John steps into the stable, he counts the calèches at the wall and spots Marie's among them. He searches his pockets for a light, in vain, then finds his lighter under the driver's bench and takes a seat in the back of his calèche.

Quietly, with the arrival of the night shift of coachmen, activity resumes. Lloyd hitches up Charogne, muttering, Chris uses the curry comb on a monster eighteen hands high, Alice slogs away at an old crackling radio, the three-legged tomcat goes by with a pigeon in its jaws .... Routine, minus one detail: Billy.

Back from Old Montreal after his day's work, Georges Prince spots a narrow space between John's yellow buggy and a heavy white "horse killer." He parks without getting out of the calèche, with grace and skill; a delicate undertaking, an undeniable sign of many years' experience. John admires his technique and the precision of every move he makes.

"So tell me, Georges, how's business in the old city?"

"Two brown bills. Starts off real quiet.... With the Kid it's always top speed. You know about it, I guess?"

"About what?"

"Well, about this nice mess: the calèche drives up against every car parked on the left. The Kid scrapes them all, one after another, all the way to the corner of the street. Ask Le Rôdeur, he was there and he would ask for nothing better than to spread the news. He said he'd never seen Champion race like that."

John realizes there's a good chance Marie's bum will never sit on a calèche seat. Most inexperienced drivers are released prematurely into the landscape. Getting the permit doesn't mean much and the tenderfeet who choose to stay in Griffintown are often just more stubborn and carefree than the others and not necessarily more talented. He has never forgotten his own first day. Back then he had to hitch up by himself and live with the consequences of his ignorance. Nervous like every driver about to launch himself for the first time onto the Bonsecours hill, John had done a good job of calculating his manoeuvre, waiting for the light to turn green so he wouldn't be stuck in the very middle of the slope, then quickly went into a trot. There was no one on the hill to impede his ascent, he was making good progress until the horse broke into a run and John couldn't understand why. Then the driver could feel that, under him, the calèche was backing up: horror, his horse was unhitched! He had jogged along to the stand by himself and John — still on board the calèche along with a family of Mexicans, who thought it was all a lot of fun — had crashed into a delivery truck.

Most of the coachmen have similar stories to keep in their closet. After an accident there are two options: give up on the thought of becoming a driver or overcome the fear, like the young rider who gets back in the saddle, trembling after a fall, and is told he has to fall seven times before he can say that he knows how to ride a horse. Honour and ego are severely scratched, but it's a necessary step.

✳ ✳ ✳

BILLY'S TROUBLES AREN'T OVER. Since his discovery the day before, he hasn't slept a wink. In the stable to feed the horses, he notices that Champion's forefeet are rigid and his hocks are sore. Walking is painful and the sight of him making his way cautiously … it's as if he has an egg lodged under every shoe. Weary and with nearly two decades of calèche driving in his bones, the old gelding no longer has Poney's stubborn vigour, Lou's pride, or Pearl's vaporous ease. When he started pulling a calèche, in Mignonne's day, when Paul came on the scene, there was already praise for his stoic temperament and his fine and friendly Belgian head. There are horses that greet one another among themselves: Champion has always been engaging. But after Mignonne died he stopped greeting his fellow creatures. The following summer, when he returned, his pace slowed and he adopted his legendary expressionless gait, the stiff and clumsy stride that exasperates the experienced drivers. This morning, the veteran's expression is even glummer. Billy stays at his side. In the spring, he was unsure for some time about whether he was or was not going to inflict one final season on him. For the new drivers, an old slow horse who knows the job is a reassuring companion. Billy knows from experience that once wear and tear have settled in, it's best not to prolong indefinitely a calèche horse's career the way another owner, Gilbert, does; he buys up at auction horses intended for meat and imposes one more summer on those tired creatures with an absent look who can't take any more. Without being unduly attached to the horses, Billy always knows when the time has come to hang up their shoes. The groom leads Champion delicately to the transport vehicle, respecting his slowness. Irritated by the pain in his feet, Champion sweeps the contaminated air of the stable with his tail one last time before plunging into the light of this early June morning. An entire chapter of calèche culture and the history of Griffintown will be extinguished with him in the grave, and a diaphanous silence will descend, a requiem for an old horse who is going to rejoin Mignonne. When he gets there he'll salute her.

* * *

JOHN GOES INTO THE stable early that morning, hoping he'll run into his protégé. He notices there is no trailer truck on the site. Spotting Champion's empty stall he realizes he was wise to come. On the board where Billy leaves notes for the drivers, he reads that Marie has inherited Poney and that he himself will take back the reins of the Haflinger, the febrile and unpredictable horse he'd started to train. This more or less suits him but under the circumstances, he'll adapt.

Georges Prince arrives early, as usual, with Marie following close behind. John sees her fling her bike into a stretch of couch grass in a grove. Calling the three-legged cat, she tries in vain to approach it. As far back as he can remember there has always been a three-legged cat in the stable, a hostile environment of the finest example where the animals often injure themselves. John saw the veterinarian amputate the wounded paw of the latest cat. He disappeared for a few days then came back, starving and wilder than ever, still a skilful hunter of fledglings, field mice, and bats, whose wings it leaves intact. Too tough. Three Legs is like a pirate with a wooden leg, similar to Evan: bitter, furious. Like him, it's bad moods that keep him alive.

John goes first with this anecdote to Marie, because she likes his stories about drivers and horses, then he announces that Champion has hung up his shoes. "Plenty other horses will leave you and break your heart, Marie. You'll come back in the spring and the one you're anticipating won't be there. Or he'll be waiting for you and you won't be back. You have to toughen up or you won't make it through the summer." Marie's little-girl pout, her long arms, like chiffon, her aching shoulders and the sadness that swept over her, remind him of the only time he's seen a driver cry, at the death of Mignonne, over her big, white, shattered body covered with a blanket that left her four shod feet sticking out. He remembers too the day Ray hanged himself. John had stepped into the stable at dawn, as usual going through the calèche garage. And he had spotted the long rope hanging from ceiling to ground, still tied around the neck of Ray, hidden under a worn wool blanket, the toes of his cowboy boots sticking out. Billy, mute and motionless, sitting on a cube of hay. And, since then, there's been a crack in the ceiling near the beam.

John pushes aside the couch grass with the toe of his boot and points out to Marie the two small crosses: Ray's, on which can be read, "Died with his boots on," and Mignonne's, two planks nailed together on which a female hand has drawn in pink the horse's name. No dates, because no one knows when either one came into the world. The couch grass that grows abundantly on their graves covers the crosses almost completely. That's the way it is in Griffintown, where generally drivers and horses sentenced to death don't last long, other lives coming to keep them out of the limelight. "There will be other horses, Marie," says John.

✳ ✳ ✳

THAT MORNING, THE ENTRANCE of Marie's ancestral calèche with Poney hitched to it attracts a lot of attention on the way into Old Montreal. On rue Notre-Dame the blue-collar workers have removed the metal plate that was the cause of Champion's accident. Marie vows that she will get through this day.

"Hey!" shouts Alice across the street in front of the Basilica. "That horse isn't for little girls!" Marie stops a little farther along, at the top of Place Jacques-Cartier, at the stand with the fewest customers. This morning she is the first arrival and doesn't need to make her horse back up, which suits her. John told her that making the calèche back up is like playing pool, that she just needs to understand the angle for lining up calèche and horse and, afterwards, it will go almost by itself, it comes with practice. But Marie doesn't know how to play pool. She offers a carrot to Poney, who savours it without dropping a crumb, efficient even in the way he devours treats. On her way to the drinking trough she spots Le Rôdeur, who is approaching.

"So, Kid, you managed to get here in one piece. Coffee?"

Shortly after, she experiences the drivers' quantum law, which John had already told her about: "Soon as you've got a coffee in your hands, you take on your first customers, without even appealing to tourists." Out of pride and so as not to worry them she doesn't tell a couple of fiftyish Torontonians that they are her first passengers.

Seeing that she's taken on her first client before him, Alice grins sardonically. Marie's attention is focussed on what road to take, the dates to remember, and the description of architectural styles. The Aldred Building, the one that's shaped like a wedding cake, is art deco. The National Bank and its impressive outside vault that's protected by a tangle of electric wires are visible from rue Saint-Jacques. Paul de Chomedey de Maisonneuve, the guy with a pigeon on either shoulder in the very heart of the Place d'Armes: founder of the city in 1642. The Saint-James, with its suite that goes for five thousand dollars a night where Mick Jagger stayed.... All is well. Poney turns out to be the ideal companion. Turning onto rue des Recollets, she hits the corner of the sidewalk; her tire elastic comes undone. Fortunately, she's not in the field of vision of any driver. After telling the tourists she needs a couple of minutes, Marie gets down and tries in vain to repeat what Billy did after the accident. With no elastic, she gives the impression of trotting along in a dilapidated carriole along a bumpy road. She can't help it, she has to come up with a way to tighten the elastic. For it to work she has to be able to lift the calèche for a fraction of a second; the task seems to her impossible. It lacks a third hand.

Georges Prince passes close to her with the Clydesdale still hitched to the green buggy adorned with stuffed animals and roses. The mare lopes along, her strides so long that her walking speed is nearly equal to the working trot — in fact, she seems out of breath and has a little foam on her lips. The star driver waves at Marie and then, without even smiling or interrupting his explanations to the people seated in his calèche, he jumps out, joins the young driver, fixes the tire elastic in a quarter of a second. Gentlemanly, he gives her a wink and leaves with no further ado.

When she reaches rue de la Commune, Marie recognizes Trudy and two other female drivers to whom she is about to say hello when a chorus of bitter voices rises up.

"Are you the new kid who wears out the horses?"

Immediately, tears come to Marie's eyes.

"It was the metal plate," she mumbles so faintly that no one hears her.

"You have to learn a horse isn't a car," one of the three women bellows.

"Yeah, you can't go to the garage to change some parts after an accident. Didn't John explain that?"

"Anyway, you aren't finished with us."

Marie inhales, exhales; struggles to get back the upper hand. There are tourists on board, after all.

"Who are those scary bitches?" asks the woman.

"My colleagues," replies Marie, looking down.

Quai de l'Horloge, Accueil Bonneau, the drop-in place for homeless men, the city's first brothel, the École de cirque: the tour is coming to an end and the convoy turns onto Berri, the street that marks the eastern boundary of the Far Ouest.

Her life on the other side doesn't interest her now. After her ex cleared out the apartment, not much was left — a lot of dust, the spice rack, and a jar of gherkins in the refrigerator. Only emptiness and the possibility of a fresh start.

The traffic light turns green and Poney, trotting, darts onto the Bonsecours hill. Then Marie does something she'd never have allowed herself as a rider: she loosens the reins and delegates all power to the animal. "Your horse is amazing," says the woman once they have come to the top of the slope. Marie thinks back to the idea of "a horse for experienced drivers." Bullshit! These horses are so sensible, so independent, they allow the driver to light a cigarette and drive with one hand, thinking about something else.

After the tourists have gone, Marie gives Poney three big carrots and a handful of peppermints. She would like to press herself against his shoulder, wrap her arms around his neck, plant a kiss on the rosette at the very top of his nose; but knowing his temperament she has a sense that those movements would unnerve him. And so she plants herself in front of him and looks him deep in the eyes.

Black and gleaming, protected by a fine ring of russet eyelashes, Poney's eyes shine with intelligence that's both sensitive and intuitive. In their depths, Marie detects something as yet untamed. Are the eyes of horses ancient jewels? she wonders.

* * *

IN HIS MUSTARD-COLOURED buggy John arrives at Marie's stand, holding the Haflinger with short reins. The biceps in his long thin arms stand out, on the verge of trembling.

Unlike Poney's, the Haflinger's ears are very mobile. Nostrils dilated, blond mane blowing in the wind, shadow of foam at the corners of his lips, the animal looks agitated and nervous, his disposition explosive.

"I'm always digging my heels in. He reminds me of my father."

Frowning, John scans the horizon and curses.

"Alice is coming to steal our gun, that's all we need!"

"Who's we?"

"He's going to squeeze himself in at the end of the line and steal our customer."

For Alice to indulge in such a despicable act is outrageous to John.

"I'm bored at the Basilica; there's been nothing for two hours," he tells John, his expression contrite. "Lloyd's asleep and I don't even have half a bell yet."

"We'll remember your tremendous talent, Alice."

Farther west on Notre-Dame, Trish, Trudy, and Patty, all of them hitched to Belgians, advance in a near-military procession towards the stand.

"The old hides!" announces John.

"Kid, you're in deep shit," warns Alice, who has just had a ride stolen for the third time.

Poney takes in the odour of the three women and their horses before he spots them: two mares and a mature gelding. From him comes a quick, cheerful whinny, a greeting that is friendly but polite, a simple expression of complicity that doesn't ask to be answered. The three horses (manes washed, coats smoothed) point their ears in his direction and take up their positions in front of Alice's horse.

The female drivers, carrying buckets, jump out in one motion and pretend they are heading for the water pump while they loiter in the space occupied by Marie. They are trying hard to catch her doing something wrong, but the asphalt around Poney is clean, the calèche is the proper distance from the sidewalk, the uprights of the bridle are tight enough, there isn't a hint of a small apple-size piece of manure in the diaper; Marie has taken the time to clean the eyes and nostrils of her horse with a cloth and to braid his black mane, using a technique that Trish, Trudy, and Patty aren't familiar with.

"It's not as complicated as it looks and it lasts all day," says Marie when she notices the other three taking an interest in the braid. "And when it's hot out it frees the neck."

John can't get over it; the Kid has been able to avoid the wrath of the main female drivers. From his bench, he watches Marie: slender, milky complexion, constant effervescence, long swanlike neck, slightly awkward. She's not so innocent and is much more enigmatic than he'd thought at first. Her gaze is open and expansive, so deep one can imagine diving into it. But not everything is so simple. There is something untamed and broken within her. She's like the horses around her: her past now haunts her. Sensing the insistence in his gaze, the young driver turns towards John, lets go of the tuft of mane hair she is holding.

* * *

TWO O'CLOCK AT THE stable, dead calm: all the daytime drivers are out and several hours will pass before the relief crew arrives in late afternoon. Billy generally uses this time to clean the stall, count the cubes of hay, sweep the aisle, recharge the batteries in the lanterns for the calèches .... But Paul's death and the discovery of his truck in the parking lot sows anarchy in his routine. He now spends a lot of time leading the investigation. The last Irishman sits on the roof of his trailer or on the freezer in the cellar, the barrel of the rifle across his lap. There he does his exercises in extrapolation that take him back to the two men. Evan, first of all, because of the madness that haunts his gaze and his megalomaniacal ideas. And Le Rôdeur, whose motivations he can't really grasp, nor his comings and goings, who spends a lot of time in the stable, in the stall that serves as his shelter. He disappears, then comes back, never giving details. In a notebook above the old billy goat's head with its gold teeth, Billy has drawn a question mark.

The last Irishman showed John the charred remains of Paul Despatie's pickup and discussed the two suspects with him, but the driver is no further ahead than he is and can at best serve as confidant. In the Saloon, the horsemen continue to get drunk and suspect one another. They're not much help either and Billy was afraid matters would get out of hand, but their usual concerns won out: the Amphi-Bus that scared the new horses; the shoes that clicked unevenly; the construction work. He trusts only one other person but he doesn't know at the moment if she is still alive and breathing, and to find her he'll have to manage by himself. Paul can't stay eternally bent double in the freezer.

He goes down to the cellar, lays the hunting rifle on the ground against a dried-up old harness on which a litter of new-born baby rats is squealing, and pulls the freezer door ajar.

When he sees Paul's head, the nape of his neck and his still frizzy dark hair, he feels as if his former boss is going to turn towards him and tell him to get Cinderella's coach ready for a wedding. Painfully, he hoists the body out of the freezer, lays it on the ground, on a tarp. He'll wait for a thaw to carry out his plan.

La Mère. He has to get in touch with her. If she is still alive.

✳ ✳ ✳

PAUL DESPATIE'S BODY TAKES several days to thaw completely. They pass like this: John happens to run into Marie at the stand, giving her as usual an incredulous half-smile; Marie amassing fares so quickly she has barely enough time to gulp a sandwich; Le Rôdeur wandering from stand to stand, carrying his brown bag; the three female horsewomen of the Apocalypse stationed on rue de la Commune near the Pointe-à-Callière; Poney and the Haflinger, each in his own way, delivering the best of themselves. Around four p.m. the whole gang sets off for home. The honeyed light of late afternoon breaks through the dimness of the stable, casting on the men's skin and animals' hide a stubborn luminosity that magnifies the scene.

On the day in question, someone has managed to tune in a radio station that comes in clearly, playing American country. Hank Williams, Leadbelly, Patsy Cline .... Listening to them — one hand on the shoulder of a horse and the other holding a cold beer, worn by the sun and filthy from the dust of Griffintown — restores the essential meaning of all this music opening up the horizons of those who slave away.

"How many bells?" John inquires.

"Two," Marie lies, when under her bench she has a little more than three hundred dollars.

"Keep a low profile when you're taking in a whole lot of cash. It's not the same for everybody and the others will be mad at you, especially at first." John himself had taught it to her. Her own trips happen in the early morning, before the arrival of the lemon-green calèche hitched to the matte-gold horse and the other drivers, while she reigns practically alone in the tourist area with Le Rôdeur as her accomplice, always wearing the jacket ripped off from a city employee. She has him board the calèche as she leaves the stable and drives him to the Old Town; in exchange he shuts his eyes when she welcomes customers at places other than her stand. After that John arrives, then the others. Already she has close to a bell, a hundred dollars, in her pocket. At night, back home in the Far East, Marie's sleep is agitated and not really refreshing. It's her own voice that wakes her in the middle of the night. She hears herself tell the story of the Centaur Theatre, formerly the Montreal Stock Exchange, a building erected early in the twentieth century, very imposing with its six columns rising in front of the facade. Eyes closed, she declaims like a robot the history of the town, face turned towards the window at the head of her bed, repeating what she has recounted at least six or seven times in the course of the day. She sees herself in a dream as well, sometimes on board her calèche but sitting on the passenger seat, stretched out uncomfortably: feet on one of the seats, knees folded like an accordion, shoulders on the other bench and neck twisted, legs dangling, trying to resist gravity.... She wakes with a start, just as she is about to fall. Her dreams exhaust her.

* * *

CROUCHING NEXT TO PAUL, Billy takes the hand of his former boss, touches his palm, and, with his own thumb, presses to see if the body has thawed. The corpse discharges a quantity of water and a small funereal mist that smells of moss and mushrooms.

The body will be waked that night, in Paul's office. John helps Billy carry Paul's sodden remains to the sofa. The very heavy legs that seemed at first hard to unfold after spending several weeks frozen in an impossible position now seem out of alignment with the trunk, as if Paul had tried to grow taller to see over a fence. He'd been shot twice in the chest; the bullets are in a line straight to the heart. Paul's complexion is a strange mauve, speckled with yellow, his hair, shaggy and oily, his fingers claw-like, his lips stretched in a sardonic grin at once grotesque and cynical.... John casts a perplexed look at the corpse.

"We got to make him look better than that."

While Billy shoves Paul's feet into his black boots and again pulls on his own, John snaps open the office latch. He remembers there's a crucifix above the door and he wants to slip it between his fingers, not having a rosary handy.

The door gives way more easily than expected. Inside, in the amber light that seeps through the horizontal blind dances in a fine but concentrated gold-coloured dust as it does everywhere in Griffintown. John coughs slightly, then smiles at the sight of Paul's cup, which is inscribed, I like my beer cold and my women hot. Paul also liked draft horses, Garth Brooks records, and western accessories. He liked to think he was a cowboy. At the bottom of his cup, in two or three centimetres of curdled milk and coffee, some sugar-mad flies have drowned.

Billy screws a candle into the neck of a beer bottle and announces that they will wake the body early that afternoon and that no horse or calèche will go out into the Old City, except maybe at the end of the evening.

John seats himself on a wooden chair, to the left of the corpse. To give himself an impression of composure and to mark the passing of time, he cracks his knuckles every fifteen minutes. On the right of the remains, Billy cleans the grime out of his nails with a pocket knife and now and then swigs some vodka. The bottle is behind the sofa, in precarious balance on the radiator. He offers it to John who, given the time, turns it down. And, like that, they await the arrival of the first coachmen while on the TV in the background come thick and fast the morning programs featuring interior decoration and cooking. On the menu: lacquered duck; truffle oil mousse; anise sherbet. On the other network a lady has saved up a thousand dollars to set up a small feng shui boudoir. Billy looks at Paul, then at John, who is biting his nails, and the lady on television who is bemoaning her life over a small pile of rocks in a glass bowl. He wonders what crazy world he's living in.

They wake the corpse all day long. The coachmen cross themselves and go to sit on the bales of hay outside, right where Evan parked his trailer some weeks earlier before he disappeared, God only knows where. Lloyd has heard that he's working in an animal auction house not far from the American border. The Chinese man from the corner store comes several times to deliver cases of beer to the coachmen. In the afternoon, a squabble breaks out between Alice and the Indian. It's about Trish, busily making coffee in the kitchen. Something happened between her and the Indian during the past few days that annoys Alice, who dated her several years earlier. With cheeks purple, he rises and provokes the Indian by calling him "savage." Best not to press that button. All the alcohol soaked up since early morning has dulled their actions, slowed their movement, and muddled the precision of the blows they've dealt. John orders them to fight somewhere else, near the stream, beneath the big oak. Under the Indian's boots the earth crumbles as he draws back, in the spot where the ground starts to slope steeply towards the stream of stagnant water. He flaps his arms as if to restore his balance. He tries to clutch a branch, in vain, instead grabs Alice's arm, dragging him along as he falls. The stream is much deeper than the drivers imagine. Something like the height of two men standing one on top of the other.

The water, opaque as tar, conceals the reference points; fingers in search of something to hold on to collide with the sludgy walls covered with dead water weeds. Alice leans on the Indian's shoulder and propels himself to the surface.

The Indian reappears a minute later and it's as if they have just been born into the world. Two brothers expelled from the matrix of a black womb. One night, unbeknownst to anyone, Evan pitched a dead horse into this stream. The horse was swallowed by the water and by the creatures who live perhaps at the very bottom, have lived there from the dawn of time. The Men from the City count on the presence of this waterway to attract buyers and sell them Project Griffin-town 2.0.

When Billy steps out of the office to announce what comes next in the ceremony, Alice and the Indian have already forgotten what the dispute was about.

"We'll hitch up the calèches and the black horses," Billy announces.

"What about Paul, what do we do with him?" asks Lloyd.

"In the buggy that takes people on rides to the sugar shack. Needs a cleanup, a scrub to get rid of the mildew and cobwebs. La Grande Folle is coming."

They adorn horses and calèches, straighten the equipment, and transport Paul's remains in the biggest calèche, hitched to four Percherons made light-headed by the manoeuvre. Shortly afterwards, an unruly procession turns onto the streets of Griffintown: five calèches in all, some twenty drivers and Le Rôdeur following, playing the harmonica. La Grande Folle brings up the rear, also on foot. The horses are nervous because the drivers are shouting and still drinking, bottles are smashed on the asphalt, and the sound of horseshoes smashing glass worries Charlie in the four-way harness; he starts to gallop slantwise, forcing the other horses that are hitched up to follow him, and the calèche seems about to capsize like a canoe. The coffin, a clattering assemblage of twisted planks, rolls off its base. The procession continues, noisy and undisciplined, the horses pounding the ground with their shoes, sweeping the air with their short Percheron tails, ears twitching, breathing gusts of moist air through their nostrils while the drivers recall the summer when they'd all got a dose that made them piss green. A memory more or less appropriate given the circumstances, but at least they're making noise. Their convoy doesn't go unnoticed and that's part of Billy's plan.

As anticipated, La Mère sees them go past, La Mouche, too. The first is perched on the roof of a neighbouring building, the second is taking refuge behind a porte cochère.

Back at the stable, Billy sends the coachmen home and waits. An hour passes, then two. Paul's makeshift coffin has been set down on some bales of hay. Billy wonders once again how to dispose of the body, hoping against hope he won't have to freeze it again.

No sign of La Mouche.

✳   ✳   ✳

THAT EVENING, AFTER FEEDING the horses, the last Irishman mounts Maggie and then, on her back, takes his tobacco pouch out of his shirt pocket, rolls himself a quickie, pulls down his cap, and orders Maggie towards the stream and the Lachine Canal, intending to follow it to the locks.

Not far from rue de la Montagne, through the half-open door of a small factory that makes multi-coloured suitcases, he observes the employees for a moment. Blue suitcase, then red, yellow, green, pink, all for storing who knows what, planning to go who knows where. Billy is suddenly struck by a dizzy spell. The sky is about to fall on his head and he can't escape his fate. This helplessness is unbearable.

Behind him, towering above the skyscrapers, is Mont Royal and its eternal cross, about which he's heard so many different stories, depending on which driver was telling it, to the point where he doesn't even know how it got there and most of all, why it's so important for it to stay in place. No matter what he does, it seems there is always a cross in his field of vision.

It occurs to him that people like him, who stuff corpses into freezers, are probably no longer eligible for divine aid.

Billy squints. On the horizon, starlings fly around the first small customs post not far from the locks. A fly settles on his cheek. He waves it away, aggravated. It comes back. He shakes the reins in every direction to force the animal to leave. Thinking she's dealing with an awkward command, Maggie rushes into a gallop.

He lets her go on. Maggie enjoys the damp carpet of plants, soft beneath her hooves; she speeds up, lengthens her stride, and her mane is tousled, lifting up and dropping down. Once he has reached the locks, Billy pulls on Maggie's reins, makes her slow down, then brings her to a halt. He ties her to a lamppost, making a knot in the reins. The starlings are still chattering.

Wondering why they're so excited, the groom jumps out, bending his knees — a trick so the pain of impact won't crack his kneecaps in two — and approaches the handrail. In the water that is largely responsible for the starlings' turmoil, a red ball with yellow polka dots is swirling at the bottom of a small cascade, kept in place by the current that catches up with the falls in the opposite direction: stagnation in motion. He lets out an oath. Hearing him, Maggie raises her neck, orients her elegant head towards him, stops chewing, and slowly blinks. The grace of a horse, its singular vision, is enough at times to interrupt the man in his mute soliloquy.

They take the same route back to the stable. The mare drags her feet a little, giving Billy time to roll a second cigarette; he cracks a match, creases his eyes, approaches the flame and inhales deeply, replacing the knot in the reins balanced on the pommel of the saddle. In the distance, the tin castle appears to be about to collapse. There must be a limit to the patching-up, a point of non-return, a moment when forced to throw in the towel and give up before the effect of time, before the work of gravity and erosion. The material bends, splits, falls apart, scatters, and that certainty gives Billy an urge to swallow a handful of earth; he feels the sand crumble, become dust between his molars, all the way to his belly.

His attention is suddenly attracted to a dried-out, porous object; it could be coral or a crown of thorns, a dried sponge, perhaps white birds squabbling over a morsel of bread. The mass of leaves and twigs that has formed at the corner of Murray and Ottawa advances, twirling, apparently aimless, along William Street. He thinks: I'm alone in Griffintown with the horses.

After leaving the strip of the Lachine Canal, he arrives at Richmond Street, mute and desolate as ever, and stops suddenly before a scene that takes his breath away

Close to the stall used for storing hay, at the end of the aisle where Evan parked his trailer before he ran away, La Mère Despatie watches over the body of her son.

LEAD IN THE EYE

KNEELING BESIDE THE REMAINS, La Mère has set down her rifle. She unbuttons Paul's shirt, frowns. Then sticks her fingers into the wounds and extricates two bullets she holds up to the sun, which turns them red, a ball of fire in a rose-coloured sky. Two shots to the heart, the work of a pistol nearly as ancient as the old Schultz & Larsen given by her father. There's no possible doubt; the murder has been signed. La Mère slips the bullets into her pocket.

When she recognizes the groom on horseback in the distance, she whistles and gestures to him to approach, then gets up and advances towards him, her expression like Doomsday. At seventy-five, La Mère looks more than ever like a tough nut to crack and she does justice to the outlaw reputation that runs through the Despatie lineage. She has taken off the green beret she wears all the time. Her shrivelled fingers are stained with pink and liquid blood, like a bird's, Billy observes, joining her.

Though still in a state of shock, the last of the Irishmen senses he'll have to get a grip — and fast; in the presence of La Mère and Paul's body, he'd be well-advised to say something profound.

"We'll have to avenge his honour! I'm going out to track down the piece of shit that did that," he boasts, fist raised.

"Stay away from that, kid. Start by getting rid of the asshole's body. I'll deal with the rest."

Disposing, once again, of Paul Despatie's body. Billy has the unpleasant impression he's back to square one.

La Mère glances at the holes in her son's chest and continues:

"In my day, we left the men alone. We respected a kind of … of ethics. We had manners and we didn't depart from the code."

Billy has heard of the methods of the old guard. At the time, prohibited goods passed systematically between the hands of the horsemen. Quickly, clans had formed, including the Despaties. Many horses have perished in appalling slaughterhouses. According to what Billy picked up, struggles for power, horses steeping in blood-stained straw — all that had decreased, then stopped completely, when La Mère Despatie had made a pact with the Montreal mafia, yielding part of her power in exchange for their protection. Normand Despatie had just succumbed to pneumonia and La Mère had inherited some of the business, her son being still too young to take over the reins. It was the beginning of an era undoubtedly not so prosperous but a lot less bloody, one that endured for decades and would no doubt have gone on like that for years … if the mafia hadn't infiltrated the construction field and spread its roots to the planned redevelopment of the Far Ouest.

Over the past decades, after finding gold in Griffintown, La Mère sat her son on the throne and then went back to the shadows. From her hiding place, she continues to watch over the delicate union between horsemen and the men with black hats.

The Men from the City haven't beheaded the right man. How could they have made such a grotesque mistake?

They tried no doubt to lay the blame on La Mère, who is at once everywhere and nowhere; it's impossible to point a gun in her direction. Rumours about her are making the rounds: some claim she's living the good life in Cuba in a hacienda with an ocean view, others that she is living in a triplex in Pointe-Saint-Charles next door to a Polish shop. Joe is sure he spotted her at the Bingo Masson; Dan has heard that she's taken up trafficking World War I weapons, like her father before her. Rumour has it that La Mère has bought "some shack for the rich" in Brossard near the DIX30 mall where she is enjoying a peaceful retirement watching old episodes of Bonanza and listening to her LPs of Willie Lamothe and Dolly Parton.

Fiction, fantasy, and reality are confused as in every story about coachmen, favourable breeding grounds for the birth of legends of the calibre of Laura Despatie's, a woman at once small and immense, with her rifle on her hip, her murderer's haze and her built-up boots, legacy of the polio she had contracted as a small child.

The last Irishman watches her limp away. Cursing, muttering, gripping her rifle like a cane. From now on there are two of them carrying Paul Despatie's body at arm's-length.

* * *

THE HÔTEL SALOON DISPLAYS a closed sign; it's not yet noon but already the August sun is beating down.

In the room at the back, Laura Despatie is pondering her vendetta while she chews plug tobacco and spits it on the ground. She has to reply; grief will come later. After such an affront, peace is impossible and what's to follow, a risky algebra. For now, La Mère does not grasp what they want to take from her, or communicate with her. No doubt it's a question of territory. Is it possible there's been a change of clan or regime in the Mafia? One thing for sure, they'll have to keep a sharp eye on the livestock. But can Billy really be trusted? It's been a long time since Laura Despatie has battled Evil in Griffintown; she is unfocussed and her fighter's reflexes not as sharp as they used to be.

She is still convinced of one thing: best not to under-estimate the intentions of the riffraff who ordered the murder of her son. For now, she recognizes the underling — and he'll pay for this despicable act — but not the one or ones who pulled the strings.

She oils the tip of her rifle.

✳ ✳ ✳

La Crinoline

It was said that for a number of years, before she took over the Hôtel Saloon, Laura Despatie had run a small house where businessmen and a few lawyers had appointments with prostitutes from the east end of town wearing full-skirted dresses like Claudia Cardinale. On the walls of the rooms with their rustic furniture hung lassos, whips, photos of dried-up mountains, statues of grey wood, giant cactuses, and droves of mustangs. Paul was a teenager at the time of La Crinoline; hidden in a broom closet between two rooms, he would get an eyeful through cracks he enlarged with a screwdriver and a Swiss army knife. When for reasons she would never know she was ordered to place the key under the door, she decided to open a tavern, and the bulk of the interior decoration ended up in the Hôtel Saloon. The double doors in the stairway that led to the rooms were taken down and placed in the entrance to the Saloon.

On the yellowing photos in the brothel and in the hotel, there was an eternal sky of faded bluish yellow to stare into.

A few girls from La Crinoline recycled themselves in the calèche business: Trish, Trudy, and Patty in particular, nicknamed "old skins" because of their past lives. One summer Paul had a chance to realize a teenage fantasy: finally to be in the client's place. With Trish it was several times a day: the office in the afternoon; at night in a calèche; on all fours in a haystack; stretched out on sacks of wood shavings.

The following year they avoided such excesses and kept their distance. Paul turned to Patty, the glummest happy hooker, intending to attach a smile to her lips. He succeeded, but in exchange she passed on the clap. Over the years most of the coachmen picked up a dose, too.

When La Mère took over the Hôtel Saloon, the brass hitching post at the entrance to the bar wasn't merely a pleasant anachronism; the coachmen went to the tavern regularly with their horses. Laura Despatie's hair was smooth and lush then, long before the wig.

Once, La Mère had had a slender waist, clear skin, and pink cheeks; though she'd never been clothes-conscious and was afflicted with a nasty limp that wouldn't have been tolerated in a horse. No client would have dared show disrespect to Laura Despatie. Once, only once, Dan was sent to take care of the protection money. The year after that the message from the mafia was categorical: it was La Mère they wanted to deal with. The little glass of white port that she served them and the tin of homemade nougat with pistachios and candied orange peel into which she slipped the wad of bills every month must have had something to do with it. But that was her little secret and she would take it with her to the grave.

La Mere's visits to Griffintown became more infrequent over time. She entrusted the stable to Paul; and to Dan, her grand-nephew by marriage, the tavern. It was in their best interest not to disturb her about a rickety stool leg or a horse with diarrhoea, or she would bark something like, "You let him knock back a can of Coke mixed with gin, you don't let him lie down till he shits, and now you're pissing me off over something that stupid? You asshole!"

Despotic and impossible to topple, old lady Despatie showed up at the Hôtel Saloon once a year when it was time to pay the pizzo. Peace had a price; it was part of a smooth business operation. Those people were in no mood to laugh, but they always had a word — or at least they'd once had one, until Paul was murdered — whence La Mère's confusion. Thanks to payment of the pizzo, troublesome visitors were rare and mafia-linked explosions tended to happen in other dives. The transaction between Laura Despatie and a man in a black hat took place in the office, after which the visitor left through the back door and Laura Despatie went back to the bar, giving little kicks to the chairs of customers whose backs weren't straight enough for her liking. The former manager of one of the last brothels in town swallowed a hardboiled egg, stuffed her cheek with a healthy quid of chewing tobacco, and limped away, God knows where, until the next settling of accounts.

* * *

LAURA DESPATIE'S TEETH HAVE taken on a waxy tinge after a day spent chewing tobacco and ingesting nothing but a can of tuna and some black tea.

As it is every Monday, the Hôtel Saloon is closed, yet from the window can be caught a glimpse of a yellowish gleam at the far end of the corridor — a bare bulb, its harsh, dazzling light seeming to spatter the whole room and even beyond, as if the blazing light were trying to run away from its source to contaminate the entire tavern.

* * *

AT THE SALOON, WITH the help of a soup spoon, La Mère removed the eyeballs from Boy. In those two holes there is, aside from the sensation of vertigo and the infinity that such a vision procures, a nest of spiders that use the time to run away. La Mère filled in the empty eye-sockets of old cracked leather with the two bullets she'd taken from her son's remains. She left the spoon on the counter near the stuffed horse and took the time to eat a pickled egg.

La Mère made a double knot in her shoelaces with fingers still stained with her son's blood, straightens her beret, holds her rifle against her side, and leaves the Saloon through the back door. In Griffintown not one horseshoe can be heard clacking along the pavement. Only the broken tread of Laura Despatie.

The cracks around Boy's eye-sockets are even more pronounced now that they have lead in them. With or without blinkers, the first horse sees nothing but the death of Paul. Beginning now, Griffintown can be summed up as a son sacrificed and a mother pondering her revenge.

✳ ✳ ✳

BILLY CONSIDERS BRIEFLY TOSSING Paul's body into the water of the canal. That would be idiotic. Facile, quick — but idiotic. Suddenly he has a strong urge to bang his forehead with a shovel, but he holds back. The groom has run out of resources.

Three Legs walks past, watching him from the corner of his eye. Despite his missing limb, the cat still has his feline agility; he ripples like a stream deviated from its course. Billy had kept his eyes off this cat during the first months of his three-legged life. At one point, Evan had intended to drown the cat, but was never able to catch him. There's no suffering left in that animal; his green eyes gleam, damp and triumphant, now that night has fallen.

Billy hoists Paul's body onto the wheelbarrow used for collecting dung. The thawed-out corpse is easier to fold, after all the time it spent folded like scissors in the freezer. Armed with a shovel, the groom digs the ground near the graves of Ray and Mignonne. It occurred to him again to swallow a handful of earth, but something in the damp and compact soil cut his appetite: one of Mignonne's shoes. Under the weight of the living, of their pretention, of their distraction, the earth and dust have preserved the horseshoes in death. Why do men have the habit of looking up at the sky when they seek answers to their questions, when truths are to be found buried under the heels of their boots? Billy notices that one hoof — the right front one — is shod, thinks it's strange, but fills it all in without pushing it and starts to dig down three metres.

Two hours later, with Paul finally buried, he saddles up Maggie and rides her all over Griffintown, tearing down the missing person notices he'd stuck to the hydro poles a few weeks earlier. It's not up to him to write the end of the story. He completed the chapter about himself without hindering the development of the follow-up, but what comes next rests in hands other than his.

The last Irishman lights up a contraband cigarette, thinking about a case of twelve he'll order for delivery by the Chinese man. He quickens his pace and sends Maggie galloping down Ottawa Street, like Mignonne in the opposite direction eight years earlier. You mustn't make calèche horses gallop — Billy knows this better than anyone. It wrecks shoes and hocks. But he likes the perfectly round loop that changing from a brisk pace to a gallop with no transition through a trot makes him feel. He lets his mare run until lather fine as the foam on milk rises from deep in her breast and spreads along her strong and beautiful shoulder. Billy feels Maggie bolt under his backside, between his thighs.

Then he stops, briskly, holding on to the reins, his horse nearly sitting under him, nose to the sky. If the last of the Irish knew how to smile he would do it at this exact moment.

✳ ✳ ✳

THE RETURN OF THE horse to Marie's life and the events of the past few days have stirred up memories, painful and ecstatic, against which she has begun to retaliate by the compulsive purchase of horse figurines — her favourite being a plastic Percheron intended for studying the anatomy of horses. These past days Marie has travelled across the city and bought all the trinkets that have caught her eye, from antique dealers on rue Notre-Dame and from Dollarama. Doing this has made her both content and dejected, moods that till now she thought were incompatible. Is it her recent breakup that has overwhelmed her? Who knows, she wonders more and more often, for Marie has the strong, alarming impression that the world is finally revealing itself as it is: fragile and without touchstones.

In her east-end apartment, the driver has decided that she'll create a labyrinth of little horses, a venture that inevitably ends like a game of dominoes. Horses knocked onto the marquetry floor now lying on the ground, knickknacks that have no relationship to the blocks of spirited grace perched on four legs that she's started to spend time with; something along the lines of a childhood dream safeguarded, of a memory found at the bottom of a trunk, intact.

Thinking about the coachmen, Marie helps up the horses that have collapsed. She would like to know where John, Le Rôdeur, Billy, even Alice were born, where they hail from.

To understand what attracted them, like her, to the Far Ouest. That obsession will soon force her to go beyond her depth. The state of the apartment testifies to it: empty save for an armchair, a mattress and something like a hundred figurines.

At John's place too, as at the homes of most coachmen, there is the same kind of interior decoration reduced to the basics. The coachmen have the feeling that something will happen at the end of the summer and that they will have to find another place to lay their heads. The less they weigh themselves down with, the less tedious will be the process of uprooting and re-rooting. The rare objects we encounter in their immediate environment are untouchable, nearly sacred. Billy cherishes the portrait of his mother and her old cribbage set that sits on a shelf in his trailer; for Alice, it's a penknife in the inside pocket of his leather coat; while Joe has been dragging around a broken compass that points to the west; earlier this summer, Lloyd pawned his watch on its gold chain to pay for Evan's treats and now has bitter regrets. No way to recover it now, obviously, with all the antique dealers on rue Notre-Dame who know how to assess these things. Whenever he thinks of it, indignation colours his cheeks and forces him to guzzle an invigorating swig. Le Rôdeur has nothing, needs nothing, and has been feeling better since he'd got rid of everything, as if now he no longer needs to tolerate being deprived of anything at all. The advantage, he thinks, is that once he is lying on the ground, his face buried in the mud, at least he can be certain he's not falling.

As for John, he has an old camera that belonged to his grandfather, then to his father who didn't know what to do with it. It is the only thing he fears being stolen.

✳ ✳ ✳

A Lone Cowhand Goes Roaming

One day John told Marie that he usually left his personal effects in a warehouse, since he went down to New York to sell Christmas trees. After that, he usually left on a long trip that took him farther south, where he managed to track down odd jobs until he'd had enough of selling fish and chips and corn on the cob on an American beach and considered going home to Montreal. During that time he would wander, sleep in a trailer or now and then on park benches, more because it appealed to him than from misfortune. On his return in the spring he was sometimes seen dozing at night in his calèche until he found an apartment not far from the stable in Griffintown and repatriated his possessions. Spring affected John like a difficult waking after a legendary night of boozing.

He had never felt like part of any group, couldn't join the ranks. As a kid he played hooky more often than was warranted. John had given up school at fourteen to stick out his thumb and head for the southern US. This renunciation arose not from a desire to bungle but from a simple sense of inadequacy around people in general. John had an undying feeling that he was a nuisance and ill-mannered — except in the presence of coachmen. Most of the horsemen felt the same thing and that may have been what explained the empathy they felt with one another. John was not exactly like Alice, Gerry, Lloyd, and company, but had told Marie this: "I've always valued those guys. They have no choice about being honest, or the strength to not be." And when she asked him about the horses, he would reply that he respected them without revering them, that most of all he liked to photograph them.

Marie had landed in Griffintown while John was trying to get away from it and, abruptly, he had an urge to snatch her from this patch of thistles. He wanted to be bound together with Marie as powerfully as she wanted to join the horses.

That detail most assuredly changed the course of history. Their own and that of Griffintown.

* * *

FALLEN FROM THE SUN, scorching drought. From the roof of his trailer, Billy spies Le Rôdeur belting eastward, a bottle of cheap whisky in his blood, cactus in his throat, a crumbly heart, rust in all his joints, creaky ankle, death rattle with every breath .... The last of the Irishmen is more and more convinced that they won't see the errand boy again after the winter; that, struggling painfully, the man is living his last season.

Le Rôdeur stumbles, pulls himself up, awkward, pitiful, panting, grimacing because of a pebble in his boot. King of nothing and serf of no one, helpful only when it suits him. He's been keeping a low profile at the calèche stands during the past weeks. The horsemen, particularly the errand boys, come and go, depending on their mood, following their lucky star or obeying their demons, slipping away only to resurface. But deep in Le Rôdeur's eyes there was a flash of madness. Something's wrong.

If he were a calèche horse he'd be sent away to make glue, thinks Billy as he guzzles his beer.

✳ ✳ ✳

ADVANCING THAT WAY FOR some time now, the errand boy runs into La Grande Folle coming along the rail line, taking her frills and ruffles to the west, red-eyed, seams of her dress about to burst, a mauve feather boa around her neck and her big purse full of sour candies. Together, and apart from the others of this world, Le Rôdeur and La Grande Folle work black magic that smells like something burning and dilates the mucus membranes in their larynxes. To them, he is on the other side of the mirror. After meeting his demon in the night, Le Rôdeur continues his epic until the blazing light of day and suddenly, on the road, when he notices her, first he squints: jean jacket, boots planted in the gravel, psychedelic skirt, long electric auburn hair with split ends, falling to the middle of her back. Upright, loving, strict, potato-coloured eyes. In short, an angel. Who holds out a hand bearing fruit.

From her cracked gaze it's easy to see that Roberta has also suffered in the past. Not so vulnerable now, she has brought a thermos of coffee to back her up and a story to tell, that of a little girl toying with the dream of a horse of her own. Impossible, because her parents didn't have two cents to rub together. But the little girl had managed to saddle a cow and mount it; she took it all over the village and everyone had a good laugh. In the fields, when the cow began to canter, with a look that was sheepish and rather grotesque, the little girl closed her eyes and imagined she was on the back of a purebred.

"That little girl is me," declares Roberta.

Le Rôdeur sobs in spite of himself, begging her to leave him alone. He's coming down from speed.

"No," says Roberta, "I just came to say you're not alone."

Exhausted, he gives up and agrees to follow her wherever she wants to take him. Twenty minutes later they arrive at the Mission.

✳ ✳ ✳

A BED JUST FOR him. Lying down, Le Rôdeur feels as if his bony carcass is going to fall apart; he has slept sitting up for fifteen years now and doesn't ask himself any questions: one eye open, one ear pricked. On this bed he's been given, stretched out as in a coffin, he dozes off in the middle of a small, window-less room, its door closed, so that when he wakes up, he has no idea what time it is; then he thinks he's dead or in jail or a police station. Roberta's voice reminds him that an angel has been watching over his destiny ever since he escaped from the Far Ouest and now that angel wants to know his name.

To tell Roberta his age would be easier: forty-five, looks sixty. He must go back to a far-off time now misted over, a tightrope walker on his own timeline. When he starts to sit down, a flash of pain shoots through his face. Roberta arranges a pillow behind his back.

"Léopold. That's what they call me," he declares in an expressionless voice.

The words jostle together in his throat as if saying his name were painful.

Roberta offers him a tin cup with good hot coffee; he agrees to eat a little — a bit of bread, some ham, a ripe pear —

while she explains that he is in a homeless shelter. With the small amount of pride he still possesses he has never before thought of himself as homeless.

In the shower the fine shell that envelopes him cracks, then gives way. Le Rôdeur melts under the scalding water, leaving all the room for Léopold, skin pink and streaming.

They give him a razor; his long salt-and-pepper beard is dealt with. As best he can, Léopold trims the bushy hairs in his side whiskers, disciplines them with a small black plastic comb from the kit that also contains a toothbrush and tooth-paste, soap, shaving gel, nail clippers, matches and a sports deodorant. Roberta gives him a few coupons for the canteen. She is still at his disposal. He's not required to say anything to her, but she knows he's there and, for the time being, that's enough. She says she worries about him. Léopold spends his days thinking about a remark he thinks is beautiful, intox-icating even: "I care about you." In bins of clothes available to the homeless he unearths a perfectly worn-in cowboy hat that would make the Griffintown coachmen green with envy.

A doctor comes to examine Léopold, especially his throat. A nurse unplugs his ears with a syringe. Clots of wax the size of small pebbles emerge. Over the following days, Léopold feels under attack by the volume of the rumbling all around: sounds of footsteps, men's murmurs, clinking keys, car traffic, ambulance sirens, police cars, fire engines: he could be for-given for thinking tragedy might strike in five minutes, that the whole city is being torn apart. Smoking a cigarette with Roberta, he hears the crackling of the fire as it burns the tobacco she inhales. His accomplice has lips as fine as rolling paper.

She helped him find a casual job as night watchman in an office tower. With his first pay he bought a bike from a junkie around Square Viger and offered it to Roberta, who quickly turned it down. She reminds him that if he wants to make her happy he just has to tell her something he remembers from his childhood, as she had done with her story of a broken-in cow.

"No cows in my story, no poor relations. Orphanage, prayers, a shelter. And a teacher who grips me hard when he sticks it in me in the dormitory."

Suddenly Roberta's eyes become ochre and bright.

"Go on, Léopold."

He lets it all out. His childhood spat in words that burn, leaving blisters on the roof of his mouth. He feels as if insects are running along his pharynx and shooting invisible stings into his throat. He has a feeling that he now has finished roving. In a few weeks he will be diagnosed with cancer of the throat.

✳ ✳ ✳

MARIE CALLS JOHN, IN her head for a start. A grey day, face silky with mist. They won't be able to hitch up today. She phones Billy to be sure, then John, presumably to inform him. She finds the courage to invite him to her place. They've never seen one another outside the Far Ouest. Marie has never tried to make reality and Griffintown touch and embrace.

The coachman would like to bring something to show that he has manners. Flowers? No, too many implications. It's a bit early for a bottle of white wine so he takes along his box of photos; no doubt Marie will find them interesting.

Arriving at her place, he holds out the box and looks for a chair to sit on. There is just one easy chair right in the middle of the living room. He sits on it. Marie stands next to him.

"Would you have anything to drink?" he asks a moment later.

While she is bustling about in the kitchen, he notices the little wooden and plastic horses all around and thinks when she comes back with a bottle of vodka, two glasses and ice, that Marie has become a genuine driver, which is in part his fault; that she's been dispossessed of her belongings the better to melt into Griffintown; that she has nothing now and has already started to decline. This is something she is unaware of.

In a gulp he drains the drink she pours for him.

✳ ✳ ✳

THE BLACK-AND-WHITE photos are arranged thematically in different cardboard envelopes, the most voluminous being the years of John's calèche, a kind of more or less private photographic journal.

When he started out, he took many photos of horses, lighting them to emphasize their weight and their ancient features, their composure inherited from a time when things were done slowly and humbly, within the rules: tidy seams of heavy rope stuck by hand into harnesses give a patina to overly ornate old wooden calèches, breeding horses with total respect for their lineage. John would photograph them from a distance and in profile, then, less and less fearful or suspicious, resulting in the series, "Heads and Forequarters," outlined under various angles often determined by the degree of luminosity and its power of reflection according to the model's coat: light-coloured, dark or in between for the Belgians that were often warm chestnut. His attention was then drawn to the eyes of the horses, their ears and their powerful shoulders.

In the series "Objects," John likes to photograph inanimate objects that seemed to him filled with meaning. An old horse-shoe hung above the door in the small sitting room adjoining Paul's office, Boy's head and shoulders in the Hôtel Saloon, the skeleton of a little bat washed by the snow, uncovered near the thistle plant where the three-legged tomcat devours his catch and Marie puts down her bike, accidentally crushing some tiny bones, Paul's cup on which can be read: I like my beer cold and my women hot. There is a trace of lipstick on the cup. That detail makes John smile. He has also photo-graphed the crack in the ceiling where Ray decided that all his work was done. But the coachman's favourite is a bouquet of daisies he immortalized just as they were beginning deli-cately to fade. John knew how to fix the nascent weariness he'd spied at the tips of the petals that had been the harbinger of the season's end.

Over the years, after a lifelong interest in animals, John began to train his lens on the coachmen, most of whom turn out to be much less hesitant than he expected: Evan — the pre-Afghanistan one — looks something like James Dean: tanned face, cowboy jeans, and a sleeveless T-shirt that showed his collarbones and the top of his torso. Ray, standing next to a haystack, leaning on the handle of his pitchfork, offers his most beautiful toothless smile. Elsewhere Paul, taken by surprise in his office, hand up like a movie star trying to escape his photographer. Billy from the back, unaware of the photographer's presence. Trish, Trudy, and Patty like triplets trying hard to look their best, sitting erect on an old church pew near the entrance. Lloyd giving him the finger. Joe, Gerry, and Alice standing in front of the city hall, proud, their expressions vulgar. Then Evan, the post-Windigo Evan, in close-up to capture the tears tattooed on his cheek. One of the most beautiful photos in the series. They're all there. Just about. Or nearly.

"Only one missing is me," observes Marie.

"We'll take care of that. Bring a dress. We'll take the photo at the stable."

I N A SKYSCRAPER, THE Men from the City are gathered around a large oval oak table.

"We'll have to move on to Plan C."

"No way around it, gentler measures haven't worked."

"You call that gentler measures?"

"I'm talking about buying back permits from the city. Despatie couldn't have cared less. Plan A, activated two years ago and reactivated last winter, was a failure. From the word go."

The atmosphere is more tense than usual around the table where three city employees are seated along with five promoters, one of whom chairs the meeting, two men in black hats, three foremen and a secretary.

"Plan B didn't work as planned either. Apparently we didn't cut off the right head!"

"Yet we'd been assured that it was Despatie who made the business run smoothly!"

"I guess they're better organized than we thought."

The place of honour, at the centre of the table, is given to the mock-up of Project Griffintown 2.0, with its red brick condos, redesigned streets, and ornamental ponds of clear water. On the site of the stable, where the tin castle still barely stands, there are plans to build a small marina to store the boats that will sail on the waters of the Lachine Canal.

One of the contractors gets up to pour himself a glass of water. Two of the black-hatted men light cigars. Time seems long to them, they don't participate in the discussion and their presence around the table bothers those who are in the habit of carrying out only part of their mandate and don't try to know the machinery that allows each of the different links in the chain to play its part smoothly.

There are no ashtrays in the meeting room, but the men in hats have portable ones that could be taken for jewel boxes.

"What's Plan C?" asks a city employee getting anxious for it to be over.

The foreman rubs his temples briefly and speaks in very concrete terms about the worksite to be organized by late October, early November.

"We don't have time to fool around with cowboys and their old nags. We have to scatter them."

Plan C, though drastic, has the merit of being infallible.

I N THE CALÈCHE GARAGE, deserted and well-lit, a single horse, white, at the end of a chain, is wondering what he's doing there. There reigns a damp silence, a dubious kind of tranquillity and as background music on the radio, an old Woody Guthrie song.

Billy takes advantage of the rainy day to clean Paul's office, get rid of all the paperwork, clear some space, throw out whatever is lying around, especially letters that begin: Re: Buying back permit — procedures. As far as he knows his boss never had a plan to sell his calèches in spite of pressure oftentimes repeated, to a small group of promoters and city employees. On the desk Billy finds a leaflet about a horse auction in Vermont planned for September, a sign that not only did Paul have no intention of shutting down his operations and getting rid of his buggies, but that he was actually planning to acquire some new ones. John lets Billy know they've arrived and while he is readying his equipment Marie, in the harness shed, puts on a pale yellow dress, its hem dragging in the dust turned into mud. On the wall, someone has hung a distorting mirror, cracked in the centre and covered with a lacquer of sticky soot. She uses it to put on makeup.

John explains to Marie what he has in mind for the photo, nothing affected, nothing that's "too different from your regular looks, it's a portrait, don't look like you're posing." After giving her a boost, his hand glides from Marie's hip to her ankle; she points her foot. Then stretches out on the horse, head resting on the enormous Percheron rump, and drops one arm while bending her head towards the lens. John shoots this slow, languorous choreography, the full length of the leg exposed, delicate palm resting against the massive shoulder, uncombed hair spread over the horse's white hair, sleeve drooping to reveal a slender collarbone, the top of a breast: everything is done in a loaded silence filled only by the sound of the camera, the breath of the animal, and the constant murmur of the drizzle. When she swings one leg over the Percheron's neck, and finds herself sitting side-saddle, both legs on the same side, John has a hunch that something is on the point of being revealed. Until now, the faces of the coachmen and none of his other portraits — of his mother, of the owner of a fish and chips canteen, of the guy who screamed "Shoot the freak in the freakin' head" at Coney Island — have got away from him like this. Now the face slips away. Is Marie's makeup hardening her features? He wants to grasp something about her, doesn't know exactly what, but she doesn't offer it.

Then he understands: Marie has most likely lost what he's looking for as she sheds her old skin to put on the new driver's. That makes him sad and pensive for a moment. He feels responsible for her.

Between two shots, Marie brushes a lock of hair behind her ear, an unconscious gesture she repeats fifty times a day. John saw it coming and had enough time to immortalize it. "Got it," he declares, even though he was expecting more.

He puts down the camera and helps Marie back to the ground. She has never liked riding bareback, but she always savours the moment when the small of her back clings to the animal's convex flank as she gets down. John catches Marie before her foot touches the ground.

They stay like that for a moment, doing nothing, saying nothing, frozen in the excited contact of motionless bodies: a horse, a girl, and a coachman.

John hears nothing but Marie's breathing, increasingly short and heavy as he approaches her. Marie throws her head back, her feet in the mud, back leaning against the horse's warm belly. He pulls up the hem of her dress, puts his hand on her rump, and the cowboy bends over the Rose with a Broken Neck.

* * *

IN THE BACKGROUND, LA Mouche doesn't miss a beat. The moneylender waits for John and Marie to stop their to-ings and fro-ings before he gets out of the stagecoach with its wobbly wheels that serves as a hideaway for him and the other two hooligans awaiting his signal.

The last time the he spied on such a scene was when Gerry agreed to let a small amateur porno crew shoot a film in his calèche. The coachman had invited La Mouche to get an eyeful, his money's worth.

This time, he is on the wrong side; from his observation

post all he can see is a white horse with six legs.

On the opposite side, taking refuge in Rambo's stall with its view of the calèche garage, Billy sees legs wrapped around John's waist, her fine ankles, her feet covered with mud. And the imperturbable animal that serves as their support.

When the coachmen finally leave the calèche garage after shaking themselves off, they forget Rambo in the very middle of the square.

Unmoving in the swarthy light, the horse takes on the appearance of a bronze statue.

Billy leads him to his stall, delivers cubes of hay, and goes inside to fix himself something to eat.

La Mouche and his associate take advantage of his leaving to open the door of the stagecoach and leave their den.

* * *

ENTERING THE SALOON, JOHN and Marie notice immediately the two bullets inserted into Boy's eye sockets. There's just one person who can afford that kind of initiative. Laura Despatie is back and her return announces nothing good.

While he is wiping a glass, the bartender shrugs helplessly. He tosses a rag over his shoulder, joins the coachmen in front of Boy.

There is something of a robot-horse about Boy. He appears not so forgiving as before, stares harshly, pitilessly at the stage and the actors. These overpowered men, fallen into disgrace, wandering in a dying world will now have to look somewhere other than in his eyes for forgiveness and leniency.

The king is dead and buried. No one knows what will become of his patched-up kingdom. How much time now before the mended tin castle collapses on their heads? How many new horses, how many bales of inedible hay warehoused in damp stalls; how many kittens drowned in the stream; or flights of tiny bats; or envelopes slipped into the right pockets; how many one-night junkies; how many broken men and coachmen hanged; how many dirty jokes with their taste of salt; how many crucifixes above doors? How many men on reprieve have escaped? How many last chances? And most of all, who will watch over the horsemen and their livestock when even Boy has abdicated?

Not far from there, wielding torches, barbarians are advancing towards the heart of Griffintown, following La Mouche.

In the stable, the horses are starting to scrape at the soil with their hooves.

ONE LAST WHINNY
BEFORE THE ESCAPE

L AURA DESPATIE KNOWS EXACTLY where to find the man she's looking for. Not far from Leo Leonard's former stables, in the cabin of the murky parking lot where no one ever parks a car. But he's not there at the moment, so she has positioned herself at the back of a large container and is waiting for La Mouche to return.

A few metres overhead a billboard sings the praises of Project Griffintown 2.0: Peaceful, elegant lifestyle minutes from downtown. Sales Office opens in September. On the poster, a thirtyish brunette is roaring with laughter over a plate of lobster in the company of a man with greying temples, serene, wreathed in success, who seems to be behind the witty remark that has made his companion burst out laughing. Holding a glass of rosé he smiles, thinking no doubt about the happy, peaceful, elegant years that appear on the horizon.

Mignonne's ghost would feel cramped in that Griffintown.

* * *

TWENTY MINUTES EARLIER, AT nightfall, when he was heating up some soup on the single working burner, after the train and after Marie and John have left, Billy spotted La Mère through the window, recognized her by her green beret and her limping gait; all at once the sight took his breath away. He set out to follow her, at first from a distance. Laura Despatie tacked through the lanes, walked in the very middle of the street, stepped briefly into the light, then went back to her trenches. The stock of her rifle jutted out from beneath her closed umbrella. She muttered to herself; her environment seemed to vex her. Billy heard La Mère talk about "honour," about "thankless," and "pain in the ass." She has something against someone who has never learned to mind his own business. The groom deduced that she was talking about the loan shark.

Then she made her way to the abandoned parking lot, to the place where they'd burned Paul Despatie's truck. When La Mère hid behind a big container, Billy took refuge in the cab of the pickup.

✳ ✳ ✳

AFTER WHAT SEEMS LIKE eternity, La Mouche finally shows up in the parking area, escorted by the same two hooligans. The moneylender gives them something that only Billy can see: brown envelopes probably stuffed with bundles of money. The three bandits say hello, La Mouche shakes the men's hands and they leave.

The moneylender returns to his cab and spends a moment counting something, his tongue out. La Mouche wears a beige raincoat, his yellow aviator glasses and his English cap;

recognizable out of a thousand, as exasperating as ever in the eyes of Laura Despatie.

Seeing La Mère advance towards him, he thinks the same thing about her. The same gait, scatterbrained as ever, same straight black skirt and, as always, the same old rifle at her side.

"Come out if you're a man, La Mouche."

He slips the revolver into the inside pocket of his raincoat and complies.

"One of us here is one too many," announces La Mere, charging her weapon.

* * *

The Pretender

La Mouche had not always been a vile man, without honour or speech, who could be bought for not very much in exchange for a particular type of errand. Legend has it that in the past of Griffintown he had pretended to the throne and contemplated occupying the territory.

But La Mère, very active, had been able to extend her empire faster than he could his, built discreet and profitable alliances with the men in black hats — at the right time and in the right way. A number of others, such as La Mouche, had thought and hoped that she would disappear into the air after the death of her husband. But what happened was the very opposite: she became untouchable, ever more terrifying, larger than life. As of that moment, Laura Despatie rose to the rank of legend. She was decked out with a nickname,

La Mère with a capital M. At the time, La Mouche had shown a lot of interest in the calèche business — whence his name, a mockery of La Mère. But she had never wanted him to rise too high in the hierarchy because she'd once seen him beat a horse. The coachmen could slug it out among themselves as much as they wanted, but hands off the horses. Laura Despatie had assigned management of the stable to Paul and the Saloon to Dan, her son and nephew, a decision La Mouche hadn't understood when he was there, awaiting nothing else. He would never forgive her for this reversal and would seize every opportunity to enrage her.

The story of La Mouche was a gold rush that had never produced anything.

Because a person has to live, he had become a moneylender, doubly honouring his name. In the inside pocket of his raincoat he kept at all times an A.J. Aubrey .38-calibre revolver inherited from his arms-merchant father. La Mère and La Mouche were born of the same father but not the same mother. Fruit of the old man's illegitimate loves, La Mouche was the child of a whore from the east end. He had learned his father's identity on the day when the man had turned up to offer him a blue nickel revolver before disappearing from his life for good. La Mère had never wanted to believe that this filth was her brother, and for that reason, too, La Mouche vowed to get even with her even if it took a century.

In recent years, the moneylender had started doing more and more jobs in the name of the black hats, though it never kept him awake nights. From that arose a certain confusion, for the mafia, even as they were protecting the Saloon, were making every effort to bring down the stable.

When the time had come to make the head of Griffintown roll, La Mouche enjoyed playing a part. He had signed the murder: two bullets to the heart. And he had wondered if the one person able to recognize his signature was still breathing the gold-powdered air of the Far Ouest. The answer to his question was approaching him, breathing loudly, rifle in hand.

* * *

MORE AND MORE CHUBBY, the tangle of twigs and feathers stuck together with tallow, pirouettes towards them like a ghost somersaulting, light and crumbly and easily set on fire.

La Mère and La Mouche wait until the crown of foliage is out of sight before contemplating one another. Laura Despatie spits on the asphalt, takes a step towards La Mouche and establishes eye contact.

"Shouldnt've taken on my son," roars La Mère, pointing her rifle at him.

"Anyway, La Mère, your reign is over," he replies, stuffing his hand in his raincoat pocket.

For a moment the loan shark wonders where the deafening sound of the drum he can hear is coming from.

When he realizes that it's his own fly's heart, fragile, dry, and quivering, it's too late. The shot is fired before La Mouche has time to take aim at La Mère.

After she has watched him fall, La Mère, satisfied, blows

on the tip of her weapon. Laura Despatie has just honoured the memory of her son. On the asphalt, her shadow has taken on outrageous proportions.

From his hideout, Billy can see blood spreading in the shape of a heart on the moneylender's raincoat.

One bullet was all it took.

The cross on Mont Royal glows in the distance, eternal, but it's not for the salvation of souls.

* * *

AFTER STEALING LA MOUCHE'S weapon, La Mère limps offstage with the satisfaction of a job well done, not knowing that it was there, in that inhospitable parking lot, that her son ended his days too, on his knees, his hands behind his head, facing the moneylender.

His heavy body, hauled painfully to the cabin by La Mouche, then taken in an armoured car by two mobsters, flung into the canal, carried by the current all the way to the stream, spotted by La Grande Folle, folded and stowed in the freezer by a groom who didn't know what he was doing until he decided to expose it openly to alert La Mère before returning it to the secrecy of the earth.

Laura Despatie never waited for anyone at all before taking the law into her own hands and she would like that to be sufficient to re-establish an equilibrium in Griffintown, but she doubts it. At least the honour of her son has been avenged. All at once she feels very weary.

The metal tip of her old rifle is still smoking when Billy looms up like a shadow in the night, cowboy boots under his arm so as not to make a sound.

As he walks past Leo Leonard's old stables, he stops for a moment. Then pulls off his socks, sets his foot on the damp stones that are visible under the worn asphalt. Stones that travelled to Griffintown hundreds of years before in French merchant ships come in search of furs and wanting to avoid sailing underweight on an uncertain sea. In the more recent past, a streetcar passed this way.

In the distance a whinnying rises in the evening coolness. Then a second.

It seems to Billy that the horses are calling him.

* * *

THE ODD SMELL OF a wood stove working overtime or a cake of burnt earth is drifting in the air.

The closer Billy comes to the heart of Griffintown, the harder its emanations grip him by the throat and fill his mouth with a chalky taste. Suddenly a muffled roar like the noise of an old tree falling. More whinnying can be heard. At the intersection of Ottawa and William he is filled with a foreboding. He starts running towards the stable, protecting his face with his sleeve.

At first he thinks the fire must have started in the hay box. Someone — who? — must have tossed a butt away inadvertently. He has always been afraid something like that would happen. As he approaches the calèche garage, Billy realizes the extent of the inferno.

The fire is devouring the charming carved calèche. Not far from there, along the low walls, flying sparks lick the sheet metal, threatening to liquefy it, to extract from it a toxic syrup. The beams that hold up the roof of the garage have apparently been sprayed with oil; eventually they'll give way to the combustion. Some arrogant amber flames are biting the old wood along its full height.

Trying to catch his breath, Billy leaves the calèche garage and heads for the office.

A second fire is raging in the garbage can where he threw the letters from Paul Despatie, not knowing that all this paper would feed a blaze.

Out the dirty kitchen window, through the translucent grime that serves as a curtain, Billy realizes that the fire is going to overwhelm all the pavilions of the tin castle.

Panicking, he grabs the receiver off the wall phone near the entrance, dials the Saloon's number, and starts to scream.

In their stalls, the horses stamp the ground and kick at the posts that define their space, old dry wood that will burn like a match. Billy unfastens the chains that keep them captive, opens wide the door to what used to be Champion's stall where Maggie now takes her place. He grabs her by the halter, tries to pull her out, pulls on her beautiful head with all his might.

A black horse goes past the stall, panicking, fire in her mane, front legs very far apart. Despite the smoke, the groom identifies Pearl by her fleshy thighs with their coppery glints.

He hears crackling at the other end of the stable, a grave, repeated neighing, Poney, then human voices, John's, Joe's, and Alice's. Reinforcements.

The coachmen arrive just in time to see Pearl slide into the stream on folded knees. The clammy earth falls apart in layers under her hooves as she advances into the water. They also see Lloyd's Charogne rear up in the reddening light, then collide with a wheelbarrow. And that's when the power goes off, sentencing horses and coachmen to falter in the dark and in the flames like the living dead they have become.

To the flames, Pearl preferred the uncertain water. Moving away from the fire, abandoning these men, it scarcely matters on what road, leaving them seems to be the only possible way out. She turns her dark, imposing head towards the coachmen one last time, thinks about them briefly, then disappears.

* * *

MARIE STARTS OFF IN different directions, trying to see the horses in the smoke. A man's voice, Alice's, yells at her to stop that little game and get moving. She hears Billy yelling at his mare to get out of the stall, calls her mule-headed, crazy filly hamburger meat and every name that comes to mind. Marie wants to help him, even though flames are licking at her ankles, burning the lace at the hem of her dress. Even as a second voice, John's, calls to her, coughing, with a cloth over his mouth, and also orders her to get the hell out.

To save a horse: it seems to Marie that her whole life has been reaching towards this one accomplishment.

"Most of the horses are already out!" screams John when he realizes what she wants to do.

Next to her, Billy pulls at his mare's halter as hard as he can. Marie hears him moan and curse, then plead. It's hopeless; the stoical Maggie's hooves are nailed to the ground. Invisible roots have grown under the fork of her feet, in the nail, through the metal of the heated shoes. Obstinate, she'll stay there.

Arms held out before her, Marie is trying to find the groom, her mare, her way. Thinking she has finally found the stall, she collapses into the horse shower like the drowning victims who imagine themselves coming back to the surface though they are foundering in the depths, numb and deluded. A horse passes near to her, avoiding her, but from where she is now she can make out only a crimson, smoky screen. Outside can be seen the animals freed from their stalls trotting along Ottawa Street, others on William Street and still others fleeing along the bike path, whipping the air with their tails or galloping in a field that is going to make way for a construction site. Grey pebbles are stuck beneath their hooves.

Always, during a fire, a certain number of horses refuse to leave the stable, or will go back to it after they've been freed from the flames. The horsemen all know that, they sense it right away in the pit of their stomachs. They've always known it. It is not a legend or an exaggeration; for once, it's the truth. A truth that's a kick in the balls.

Billy collapses into the soiled straw on the floor; he will die by fire, under the hooves of this animal he loved to feel moving under him. The mare will let herself fall onto the groom. Their flesh will be consumed in one furious flame.

The calèche garage may survive, but the stable is so dilapidated it would be best to wait for the firemen before venturing inside. Marie has fainted in the horse shower. A beam has collapsed on her, crashing violently onto her back. Another crushes the nape of her neck. The boards of the roof have started to give way where the metal — burning hot, reddened, like lava — is no longer enough to keep them in place.

John spies a piece of yellow cotton, Marie's dress, then a

leg, and the other. The long fingers of a woman lying motionless in the embers. He will blow on her body until life is restored.

Joe and Alice see a man on fire emerging from the stable, carrying in his arms a girl whose hair is still on fire: Rose with a broken neck.

Firemen are busy around the stable. On Richmond Street a police car has collided with a horse. An ambulance arrives, along with a small veterinary team.

They drape a fire-retardant blanket over John's shoulders, and pump oxygen into his lungs; paramedics wrap his legs, arms, torso, and head in rolls of sterilized gauze. Around him in the ambulance are ointments, flasks, cries, shrieks into walkie-talkies, and, high up, the droning of a helicopter. John hears the thud and crackle of boards and beams giving way. The siren of an ambulance speeding towards the Grey Nuns' Hospital with Marie on board.

The horses can't be seen now but they can be heard galloping, panicking, in every direction. Beyond the limits of Griffintown without a bit, without a master and without blinkers, they don't know what to do with this freedom.

Together within the confines of the livestock territory, head to tail, the teeth of one resting on the withers of another, playing with their hooves and using their hocks to find a little more space, then searching again the warmth of their fellow creatures, the most peaceful horses stretch their necks to graze.

* * *

THE STABLE COLLAPSES AT dawn.

The heart of Griffintown is consumed with Billy, Poney, and Maggie inside.

On the glowing coals are the smoking skeletons of calèches, red-hot metal rods, shoes, braids of bridles, a pair of stirrups and some shedding blades, scattered among the black logs. The lingering smell of burnt rubber tire elastics has spread. The three-legged cat edges its way through wisps of smoke, meowing.

On her knees in the middle of the street, a bearded woman is crying as if she were in front of her father's coffin. La Grande Folle, her feathered cap set down beside her, hair pulled back in a hairnet, the entire contents of her purse spilled onto the sidewalk: pills, powder, blush, an assortment of artificial fingernails, garters, a rock of crack. Tears are pouring over her painted skin.

Leaving the Far Ouest, she meets a horse, a golden palomino with rose-coloured nostrils, its chest injured, dogtrotting along as though nothing has happened, an animal so beautiful, so vivid, a vision of such splendour that he aches all the way to his testicles.

La Grande Folle vows never again to set foot in Griffintown.

* * *

The Rose with a Broken Neck

It would be said that she had wanted to enter Griffintown the way one desires to sleep with someone: to satisfy an urge. But tenderfeet were never welcome on the territory.

At first she thought that plow horses' features were ugly: absolute snobbishness on the part of a former rider. She no longer liked western culture, or cowboys' horses, quarter horses, or mustangs, all of them the same chestnut colour with a white line along the nose, back as straight as a riding crop and not very tall, disposition unflappable and predictable, constantly trying to slow down, while she adored thoroughbreds eighteen hands high, the kind that throw their riders to the ground and have to be dominated. She rode like a despot, always wearing spurs, claimed she adored horses but kept them highly charged, between panic and elation. They were well advised to obey, that was how she led them, and some matched her temperament perfectly. But that wasn't the way to love horses. Around Percherons and Belgians she let her guard down. Never had she felt such empathy with animals as she had at her first contact with calèche horses. Their shoulders and overdeveloped forequarters demanded respect.

Marie had wanted to save a horse, even if it meant perishing with it.

And then she had broken her neck as if it were the mundane stem of a flower, snap. Marie had sunk into a deep coma, with no dreams of animals dependent on her for survival. No nightmares about a horse's head hoisted by a chain above a well. Without John's voice like a beacon in the blackness to call attention to the traps and to highlight the landmarks. Lost alone in this starless night, Marie sank down, very far down, as one descends into a tomb.

Three weeks later, when she emerged from that long barren dream, she felt on wakening, in every fibre, that never again would she be able to climb onto a horse. Now any movement passed through her lips and onto her eyelashes like a shudder.

Marie looked all around the room in search of her yellow dress. All she found was a faded bouquet of roses and her mother kneeling beside her.

✳ ✳ ✳

JOHN HAS BEEN PARTIALLY disfigured by the flames. With first degree burns all over his back, severe ones on his hands, on the front of his thigh and his face, the coachman is waiting. A signal or a cry, the voice of Marie. Often at night he dreams that he is on fire, immolated again, and he wakes up screaming.

The flames have tanned his face and his flesh to the colour of the skin of a bison with its fat melted off by the powerful July sun. He is half-hidden under a cowboy hat. As the heel is missing from one of his boots, he has on a running shoe in its place and is leaning on a cane. He looks like a little old man — which he hates. That's not the way he had imagined his last calèche season. Love and death were not part of the plan when he made the decision to come back to Griffintown to make some money and pay off his debts. He knocks himself senseless with bourbon and waits for a signal.

At his window, the leaves of an oak tree have changed quickly from a luminescent ochre to the colour of burnt sugar. They have started to fall. He sees autumn, in the mist, being born.

John will never try to find out what happened to the horses, especially not the Haflinger, who must have been terrified by the flames even more than by the amphibious vehicle in the tourist area. John imagines them let out to gallop, running towards the horizon at daybreak, heads held superbly, vigorously. Although he has never been as attached to them as Marie, their nobility and the ferocity that drove them could still move him when he was hungover or worn-out. He plugs his ears when he hears them whinny in terror in his memories, above all does not want to recall the echo of their uncoordinated gallop as they ran away. The stable has collapsed, the coachmen seem to have scattered, wounds were taking their time to heal, and his face, painful, is oozing a purulent fluid.

Yellow, plated with gold, amber, mica: the oak leaves now in a range of colours coming from the entire palette of the embers he had braved to rescue the Rose with a Broken Neck. He recalls, wincing, the blue sparks he walked through, treacherous, sharp as blades, much worse than the orange ones that had licked his thighs, set his clothes on fire and roasted the skin off his back. He lost his camera in the blaze; he'll never see the snaps of Marie he took that day. It would be better to stop thinking about that, to concentrate on the leaves on the tree that are freeing themselves slowly, one by one. Wait for a signal. Swallow an ounce of bourbon. Wait for the nurse. And on the best days, replace waiting with hope.

* * *

NOT ONE COACHMAN SET foot in the Saloon after the blaze. Entering the tavern, Dan notes that Laura Despatie has been there, that she's eaten a pickled egg and left the jar out again. As she did last time, she fiddles with Boy's eye sockets, which he doesn't appreciate. Boy no longer has the leaden gaze of Armageddon. Henceforth there are two holes, that's all. Only black in place of the eyes. Which is even worse, because Boy has lost all his former dignity, is now nothing but a hopeless framework speckled with dull hairs.

They'll have to take him down and hang something else on the wall; an illuminated clock for instance, or how about a new flat-screen TV? At worst, a classic deer's head.

In addition to not picking up after herself, La Mère forgot to switch off the light before she left the Saloon. "I bet she didn't even lock the door," Dan muttered to himself.

In the office, the same sticky light. Dan rarely goes in there; he does his books sitting at the bar after closing.

And that is when he sees her: sitting at his desk, her body violently twisted to the right, a bullet hole in her left temple. Blood all over, on the wall, on her, on the wooden floor near the wastebasket where she spat her chewing tobacco and missed her target four times out of five.

In front of her, Dan spots the old revolver that belongs to La Mouche, the two bullets taken out of the founding horse's eye sockets, and this note: "I don't want to know what's next. Farewell sweetheart. Don't look for me in heaven. Aunt Laura."

While taking her life, La Mère lost her beret, but her wig stayed firmly in place.

✳ ✳ ✳

HITCHED TO A WHEELCHAIR, pushed by her mother, Marie comes back to John.

He shows her the extent of his burns, minor lesions, and sores. Breaks his cane in two and asks Marie if she knows where to find a cobbler able to stick back the heel of his boot. She tells him that she knows a miraculous salve that will fade scars once the wounds have healed.

He has seen her many, many times lean over towards the horses' pasterns, spread a brown ointment over all their little sores and their slightest scratches.

"Now your skin is like leather, John."

John frowns. Marie is planning to treat him with horse medicine.

"We'll talk about horses another time, okay?"

"Yes. I've got something magnificent to show you."

She points with her chin to make him look in the direction of her right hand. The tips of her fingers — index and middle — rise for a brief moment.

"See that? Something is moving in that part of me."

She seems at once proud and exhausted.

A beautiful day. In Marie's hands, leaning against her palm, a pair of reins stretch out again. It's written in the sky, sown in the earth, inscribed in the leaflets of clover blossoms, in the DNA of the three-legged cat, in the veins of the couch grass that grows all over Griffintown.

The cross on Mount Royal can be useful when the time comes to formulate a prayer. You can rest your gaze on it and murmur very softly, "Let that girl get back on her horse."

John hopes with all his might that the electricity will come back too in the centre of Marie's body, in her sex, between her thighs, and all the way to the tips of her toes.

THE CHOIR OF REDEMPTION

GOING BACK TO THE Far Ouest, Léopold realizes that he doesn't miss the horses. The smell of wet coal and cool sheet metal float over Griffintown and interfere with his breathing. He pulls up his scarf.

The neighbourhood in November has the look of a ghost town. Crossing the border, he was expecting to come up against this silence, this defiant architecture. He has lost a lot of weight during the past months. When he spies her silhouette in a warehouse window, he does his best to straighten his spine. Despite his illness, he feels straight and dignified on the inside.

Léopold recently took part in a demonstration by the Duplessis orphans in front of the Notre-Dame Basilica. His voice joined those of a hundred broken men in a unanimous speech that carried a long way. He will be operated on during the next few weeks; Roberta has promised to be at his side. As of now, he'll no longer be alone.

He wants to say hello to the coachmen before winter reclaims its rights over the territory, followed by night, to announce to the groom that his wandering days are over, that he's finished sleeping in a stall and being known as Le Rôdeur. He is no longer the vagabond bastard with gold-plated teeth. His name is Léopold: an orphan with a medicare card, a social identity. He will not come back to Griffintown in the spring.

On Richmond Street, when he reaches the corner of Basin, Léopold hears in the distance the echo of a man's voice that puts him on guard, encourages him to turn on his heels and leave the premises. But Léopold does nothing. He thinks he has recognized Billy.

The Conquest of the West finally led to the dissolution of the small company of coachmen. The Men from the City have orchestrated the rowdy flight of the last heavy horses and driven the coachmen away once and for all. Cowboy bandits, outlaw crack smokers, and their retinue of creaking calèches have surrendered. The Men from the City have won, without getting their hands too dirty.

They quickly replaced the placards: *Attention, calèches. Slow down!* by others reading: *Coming soon: upscale building complex. Construction starts this fall. Thank you to the first buyers.* After that, they started to smother the putrid fumes by beginning to settle the matter of the stream. "That must be the kind of water drunk in hell," they told one another as they pumped out all the liquid. In the dried-up bed the Men from the City found a rusted-out pitchfork, an old TV set, a typewriter, some shards and other fragments of china, a calèche wheel, a woman's shoe, a number of bottles of spirits, a crucifix, some horseshoes, empty snail shells, soft drink cans, syringes, condoms, and, barely recognizable, the infantryman's uniform of the One who'd run into a Windigo. Thus cleaned out, the stream also released the skeleton of a horse with hundreds of small brown snakes wrapped around its sides.

As the former delivery man advances through this landscape of ruins and desolation, he hears a lament rising up. In the remains of the calèches, the ghosts of horses stumble, then unhitch themselves, move on to a parade trot in the loose stones and fallen rocks, roll around in the coal-stained grass, mix their ghostly breath with the rumbling of the neighbourhood. The song, punctuated by a blacksmith's hammer, swirls up into the carbonized air. It is a requiem in reverse. The dead who sing for the living, led by the resonant voice of Billy, the one who ordered Léopold to leave the premises.

They sing of the humanity at once frail and powerful that once reigned over Griffintown. But where will the ghosts go after this day of reckoning?

Where once Cinderella's coach intended for weddings was stored, the Men from the City have erected an indecent crane. In the calèche garage, sitting on a mound of red bricks roughly covered with a tarp, Ray the hanged man is singing too, whistling every now and then, watching Mignonne shake herself in the burnt earth.

Léopold takes from his pocket his harmonica to play with his people the last bars of a dislocated melody, the one from the last chance saloon, which he knows already by heart.

He interrupts himself and muses: "I don't want to be reincarnated as a horse."